Gustav Kobbé

Wagner's Ring of the Nibelung

Gustav Kobbé

Wagner's Ring of the Nibelung

ISBN/EAN: 9783337385972

Printed in Europe, USA, Canada, Australia, Japan

Cover: Foto ©Andreas Hilbeck / pixelio.de

More available books at **www.hansebooks.com**

WAGNER'S

RING OF THE NIBELUNG.

BY

GUSTAV KOBBÉ.

SIXTH EDITION.

NEW YORK:
G. SCHIRMER
1894.

———

— TO —

CAROLYN WHEELER KOBBÉ,

———

CONTENTS.

ILLUSTRATIONS.

LEADING MOTIVES.

NOTE.—The scores to which frequent references are made in this book are the Piano Scores, with Words (simplified edition), by R. Kleinmichel. For instance, page 25, line 1, given as a reference on page 9, means that the musical passage spoken of will be found in the first line on page 25 of the simplified edition of the Kleinmichel piano-vocal score of "Rhinegold."

PREFACE TO THE SIXTH EDITION.

THIS is the sixth edition of my "Wagner's Ring of the Nibelung" in separate form ; but, as these analyses are also part of my two volumes entitled "Wagner's Life and Works," the book may be said to have really reached its seventh edition with this issue.

I attribute this popularity—which is gratifying to me chiefly because it attests the popularity which Wagner's works have attained—to the fact that the analyses are entirely untechnical and to the numerous musical examples. They are just so many illustrations, presenting to the eye and through it to the hearing, what is described and analyzed in the text.

I trust this work has aided the public in recognizing what, not so very long ago, only a small band of pioneers recognized—that Wagner is the greatest tone-master the world has ever seen and perhaps ever will see.

GUSTAV KOBBÉ.

SUMMIT, UNION CO., N. J., July, 1894.

INTRODUCTION.

The " Ring of the Nibelung " consists of four music-dramas—" Rhinegold," the " Valkyr," "Siegfried " and the
" Dusk of the Gods." The " books " of these were written
in inverse order. Wagner made a dramatic sketch of
the Nibelung myth as early as the autumn of 1848
and between then and the autumn of 1850 he wrote
the " Death of Siegfried." This subsequently became the
" Dusk of the Gods." Meanwhile Wagner's ideas as to the
proper treatment of the myth seem to have undergone a
change. " Siegfried's Death " ended simply dramatically,
Brünnhilde leading *Siegfried* to Valhall. Afterwards
Wagner evidently conceived the purpose of connecting the
final catastrophe of his Trilogy with the Dusk of the Gods,
or end of all things, in Northern mythology, and of embody-
ing a profound truth in the action of the music-dramas.
This metaphysical significance of the work is believed to be
sufficiently explained in the brief synopsis of the plot of the
Trilogy and in the descriptive musical and dramatic analysis below.

In the autumn of 1850 when Wagner was on the point of
sketching out the music of " Siegfried's Death," he recognized that he must lead up to it with another drama, and
" Young Siegfried," afterwards " Siegfried," was the result.
This in turn he found incomplete, and finally decided to
supplement it with the " Valkyr" and " Rhinegold." This
backward *modus operandi* he explained to Liszt in a characteristic letter dated Albisbrunn, November 20, 1851.

" Rhinegold " was produced in Munich, at the *Hoftheater*

September 22, 1869; the "Valkyr," on the same stage, June 26, 1870. "Siegfried" and the "Dusk of the Gods" were not performed until 1876, when they were produced at Bayreuth.

Of the principal characters in the "Ring of the Nibelung," *Alberich*, the Nibelung, and *Wotan*, the chief of the gods, are symbolic of greed for wealth and power. This lust leads *Alberich* to renounce love—the most sacred of emotions—in order that he may rob the Rhine-daughters of the Rhinegold and forge from it the ring which is to make him all-powerful. *Wotan* by strategy obtains the ring, but, instead of returning it to the Rhine-daughters, he gives it to the giants, *Fafner* and *Fasolt* as ransom for *Freia*, the goddess of youth and beauty, whom he had promised to the giants as a reward for building Walhalla. *Alberich* has cursed the ring and all into whose possession it may come. The giants no sooner obtain it than they fall to quarreling over it and *Fafner* slays *Fasolt* and then retires to a cave in the heart of a forest where, in the form of a dragon, he guards the ring and the rest of the treasure which *Wotan* wrested from Alberich and also gave to the giants as ransom for Freia. This treasure includes the tarn-helmet, a helmet made of Rhinegold, the wearer of which can assume any guise.

Wotan having witnessed the slaying of *Fasolt*, is filled with dread lest the curse of *Alberich* be visited upon the gods. To defend Valhalla against the assaults of *Alberich* and the host of Nibelungs, he begets in union with *Erda*, the goddess of wisdom, the Valkyrs (chief among them *Brünnhilde*) who course through the air on superb chargers and bear the bodies of departed heroes to Valhalla, where they revive and aid the gods in warding off the attacks of the Nibelungs. But it is also necessary that the

curse-laden ring should be wrested from *Fafner* and restored through purely unselfish motives to the Rhine-daughters, and the curse thus lifted from the race of the gods.
None of the gods can do this because the motives would not
be entirely unselfish. Hence, *Wotan,* for a time, casts off
his divinity, and in disguise as Wälse, begets in union with
a human woman the Wälsung twins, *Siegmund* and *Sieglinde. Siegmund* he hopes will be the hero who will slay
Fafner and restore the ring to the Rhine-daughters. To
nerve him for this task, *Wotan* surrounds the Wälsungs
with numerous hardships. *Sieglinde* is forced to become
the wife of her robber *Hunding. Siegmund,* storm-driven,
seeks shelter in *Hunding's* hut, where he and his sister, recognizing one another, form an incestuous union and escape. *Hunding* overtakes them and *Wotan,* as *Siegmund*
has been guilty of a crime against the marriage vow, is
obliged, at the request of his spouse *Fricka,* the Juno of
Northern mythology, to give victory to *Hunding. Brünnhilde,* contrary to *Wotan's* command, takes pity on *Siegmund* and seeks to shield him against *Hunding.* For this
Wotan causes her to fall into a profound slumber. The
hero who will penetrate the barrier of fire with which *Wotan* has surrounded the rock upon which she slumbers can
claim her as his bride.

After *Siegmund's* death *Sieglinde* gives birth to *Siegfried,* a son of their incestuous union, who is reared by one
of the Nibelungs, *Mime,* in the forest where *Fafner* guards
the Nibelung treasure. *Mime* is seeking to weld the pieces
of *Siegmund's* sword (Nothung or Needful) in order that
Siegfried may slay *Fafner, Mime* hoping to then possess
himself of the treasure. But he cannot weld the sword. At
last *Siegfried,* learning that it was his father's weapon, welds
the pieces and slays *Fafner.* His lips having come in con-

tact with his bloody fingers, he is, through the magic power of the dragon's blood, enabled to understand the language of the birds, and a little feathery songster warns him of *Mime's* treachery. *Siegfried* slays the Nibelung and is then guided to the fiery barrier around the Valkyr rock. Penetrating this, he comes upon *Brünnhilde*, and, enraptured with her beauty, he awakens her and claims her as his bride, and she, the virgin pride of the goddess, yielding to the love of the woman, gives herself up to him. He plights his troth with the curse-laden ring which he has wrested from *Fafner.*

Siegfried goes forth in quest of adventure. On the Rhine lives the Gibichung *Gunther*, his sister *Gutrune* and their half-brother *Hagen*, the son of the Nibelung *Alberich.* *Hagen*, knowing of *Siegfried's* coming, plans his destruction in order to regain the ring for the Nibelungs. Therefore, craftily concealing *Brünnhilde's* and *Siegfried's* relations from *Gunther* he incites a longing in the latter to possess *Brünnhilde* as his bride. Carrying out a plot evolved by *Hagen*, *Gutrune* on *Siegfried's* arrival presents to him a drinking horn filled with a love-potion. *Siegfried* drinks, forgets *Brünnhilde*, and becoming enamored of *Gutrune* asks her in marriage of *Gunther.* The latter consents provided *Siegfried* will disguise himself in the Tarn-helmet as *Gunther* and lead *Brünnhilde* to him as bride. *Siegfried* readily agrees, and in the guise of *Gunther* overcomes *Brünnhilde* and delivers her to the Gibichung. But *Brünnhilde*, recognizing on *Siegfried* the ring which her conqueror had drawn from her finger, accuses him of treachery in delivering her, his own bride, to *Gunther.* The latter, unmasked and also suspicious of *Siegfried*, conspires with *Hagen* and *Brünnhilde*, who, knowing naught of the love-potion, is roused to a frenzy of hate and jealousy by *Siegfried's* treachery, to compass the young hero's death. *Hagen* slays *Siegfried* during a hunt, and then in a quarrel with *Gunther* over the ring also kills the Gibichung. Meanwhile *Brünnhilde* has learned through the Rhine-daughters of the treachery of which she and *Siegfried* have been the victims. All her jealous hatred of *Siegfried* yields to her old love for him and a passionate yearning to join him in death. She draws the ring from his finger, ignites the pyre with a torch and then, mounting her steed, plunges into the flames. One of the Rhine-daughters seizes the curse-laden ring. *Hagen* rushes into the flooding Rhine hoping to regain it, but the other Rhine-daughters grasp him and draw him down into the depths. Not only the flames of the pyre, but a glow which pervades the whole horizon illumines the scene. It is Walhalla being consumed by fire. Through love—the very emotion *Alberich* renounced in order to gain wealth and power—*Brünnhilde* has caused the old order of things to pass away and a new and better era to dawn.

The sum of all that has been written concerning the book of " The Ring of the Nibelung " is probably larger than the sum of all that has been written concerning the librettos used by all other composers in their aggregate. What can be said of the ordinary opera libretto beyond Voltaire's remark that "what is too stupid to be spoken is sung?" But "The Ring of the Nibelung" produced vehement discussion. It was attacked and defended, praised and ridiculed, extolled and condemned, And it survived all the discussion it called forth. It was the grandest fact in Wagner's career that he always triumphed. He threw his lance into the midst of his enemies and fought his way up to it. No matter how much opposition his music-dramas excited, they found their way into the repertoire of the leading opera houses of Germany and have since their production proved the most popular musico-dramatic works of the time.

It was contended on many sides that a book like " The Ring of the Nibelung" could not be set to music. Certainly it could not be after the fashion of an ordinary opera. Perhaps people were so accustomed to the books of nonsense which figured as opera librettos that they thought "The Ring of the Nibelung " was so great a work that its action and climaxes were beyond the scope of musical expression. For such, Wagner has placed music on a higher level. He has shown that music makes a great drama greater.

One of the most remarkable features of Wagner's works is the author's absorption of the traits of the times of which he wrote. He seems to have gone back to the very time in which the scene of the music-drama is laid and to have himself lived through the events in his plot. Hans Sachs could not have left a more faithful portrayal of life in the Nuremberg of his day than Wagner has given us in "Die Meistersinger." In " The Ring of the Nibelung " he has done more—he has absorbed an imaginary epoch ; lived over the days of gods and demigods ; infused life into mythological figures. "The Rhinegold," which is full of varied interest from its first note to its last, deals entirely with beings of mythology. They are presented true to life —if that expression may be used in connection with beings that never lived—that is to say, they are so vividly drawn that we forget such beings never lived, and take as much interest in their doings and sayings as if they were lifelike reproductions of historical characters. Was there ever a love scene more thrilling than that between *Siegmund* and *Sieglinde?* It represents the gradations of the love of two souls from its first awakening to its rapturous greeting in full self-consciousness. No one stops to think during that impassioned scene that the close relationship between *Siegmund* and *Sieglinde* would in these days have been a bar to their legal union. For all we know, in those moments when the impassioned music of that scene whirls us away in its resistless current, not a drop of related blood courses through their veins. This is a sufficient answer to the sermons that have been preached against the immorality of this scene. Moreover, as it is by no means dramatically necessary that *Siegmund* and *Siegliende* should be brother and sister, those who hold mythological beings to as strict a moral accountability as they do the people of to-day can imagine that the lovers were strangers or second cousins or anything else—only let them stop preaching sermons. It has been said that we could not be interested in mythological beings—that "The Ring of the Nibelung" lacked human interest. In reply, I say that wonderful as is the first act of "The Valkyr," there is nothing in it to compare in wild and lofty beauty with the last act of that music-drama—especially the scene between *Brünnhilde* and *Wotan*.

That there are faults of dramatic construction in "The Ring of the Nibelungen" I admit. I have not hesitated to point them out. But there are faults of construction in Shakespeare. What would be the critical verdict if "Hamlet" were now to have its first performance in the exact form in which Shakespeare left it? With all its faults of dramatic construction "The Ring of the Nibelung" is a remarkable drama, full of life and action and logically developed, the events leading up to superb climaxes. Wagner was doubly inspired. He was both a great dramatist and a great musician.

The chief faults of dramatic construction of which Wagner was guilty in "The Ring of the Nibelung" are certain unduly prolonged scenes which are merely episodical—that is unnecessary to the development of the plot so that they delay the action and weary the audience to a point which endangers the success of the really sublime portions of the score. Such are the scenes between *Wotan* and *Fricka* and *Wotan* and *Brünnhilde* in the second act of the "Valkyr"; between *Wotan* and *Mime* in the first act of "Siegfried"; between *Wotan* and *Erda* in the third act of "Siegfried"; and the *Norn* scene in the "Dusk of the Gods." In several of these scenes there is a great amount of narrative, the story of events with which we have become familiar being retold in detail although some incidents which connect the plot of the particular music-drama with that of the preceding one are also related. But, as narrative on the stage makes little impression, and, when it is sung perhaps none at all, because it cannot be well understood, it would seem as if prefaces to the libretti could have taken the place of these narratives. Certain it is that these long drawn-out scenes did more to retard the popular recognition of Wagner's genius than the activity of hostile critics and musicians. Still, it should be remembered that nowhere, except at Bayreuth, are these music-dramas given as they should be, and that they were composed for performance under the ideal circumstances which prevail there. At Bayreuth the performances begin in the afternoon and there are long waits between the acts, during which you can refresh yourself by a stroll or by the more mundane pleasures of the table. Then, after an hour's relaxation of the mind and of the sense of hearing, you are ready to hear another act. Under these agreeable conditions the faults of dramatic construction are not fatigueing because one remains sufficiently fresh to enjoy the music of the dramatically faulty scenes. Even poor old *Wotan's* frequent outbursts of grief are not nearly so tedious as they are when the " Ring" is performed elsewhere than at Bayreuth.

Wotan, except in the noble scene with *Brünnhilde* in the finale of " The Valkyr," is a bore. He is Wagner's one failure—and Wagner's failure was on as colossal a scale as his successes were. *Wotan* is the chief of the gods, a race marked out by fate for annihilation. Walking in the shadow of impending destruction he would, one might suppose, bear himself with a certain tragic dignity. Instead of this, however, he is constantly bemoaning his fate and hence strikes one as contemptible rather than as tragic. Moreover, even if his outbursts of grief were tragic instead of ridiculous and wearisome, we could hardly clothe with god-like dignity a character who pursues the female sex—divine, semidivine and purely human—with the persistency of a mythological Mormon and has reared a numerous family each member of which would probably find considerable difficulty in identifying his or her mother.

But if *Wotan* is a failure, *Brünnhilde* is on the other hand Wagner's noblest creation. She takes upon herself the sins of the gods and the Nibelungs and by her expiation frees the world from the curse of lust for wealth and power. She is a perfect dramatic incarnation of the profound and beautiful metaphysical argument upon which the plot of the " Ring of the Nibelung " is based.

"THE RING

OF THE

RIBELUNG."

"THE RHINEGOLD."

IN " The Rhinegold" we meet with supernatural beings of German mythology—the Rhinedaughters *Woglinde*, *Wellgunde* and *Flosshilde*, whose duty it is to guard the precious Rhinegold ; *Wotan*, the chief of the Gods ; his spouse *Fricka* ; *Loge*, the God of Fire (the diplomat of Walhalla) ; *Freia*, the Goddess of Youth and Beauty ; her brothers *Donner* and *Froh* ; *Erda*, the all-wise woman ; the giants *Fafner* and *Fasolt* ; *Alberich* and *Mime* of the race of Nibelungs, cunning, treacherous gnomes who dwell in Nibelheim in the bowels of the earth.

The first scene of "Rhinegold" is laid on the Rhine, where the Rhinedaughters guard the Rhinegold.

The work opens with a wonderfully descriptive prelude, which depicts with marvelous art (marvelous because so simple) the transition from the quietude of the water-depths to the wavy life of the Rhinedaughters. The double basses intone E flat. Only this note is heard during four bars. Then three contra bassoons add a B flat. The chord, thus formed, sounds until the 136th bar. With the sixteenth bar there flows over this seemingly immovable triad, as the current of a river flows over its immovable bed, the MOTIVE OF THE RHINE:

1.

A horn intones this Motive. Then one horn after another takes it up until its wave-like tones are heard on the eight horns. On the flowing accompaniment of the 'cellos the Motive is carried to the woodwind. It rises higher and higher, the other strings successively joining in the accompaniment, which now flows on in gentle undulations until the Motive is heard on the high notes of the woodwind, while the violins have joined in the accompaniment. When the theme thus seems to have stirred the waters from their depth to their surface the curtain rises.

The scene shows the bed and flowing waters of the Rhine, the light of day reaching the depths only as a greenish twilight. The current flows on over rugged rocks and through dark chasms.

Woglinde is circling gracefully around the central ridge of rock. To an accompaniment as wavy as the waters through which she swims, she sings the much-discussed

> Weia! Waga! Woge, du Welle,
> Walle zur Wiege! Wagala weia!
> Wallala, Weiala weia!

Some of these words belong to what may be termed the language of the Rhinedaughters. Looked at in print they seem odd, perhaps even ridiculous. When, however, they are sung to the melody of the Rhinedaughters they have a wavy grace which is simply entrancing. The Motive to which they are sung (Kleinmichel piano score with words, page 5, line 4; see also page 25, line 1), I call the Motive of the Rhinedaughters.

In wavy sport the Rhinedaughters dart from cliff to cliff. Meanwhile *Alberich* has clambered from the depths up to one of the cliffs, and watches, while standing in its shadow, the gambols of the Rhinedaughters. As he speaks to them there is a momentary harshness in the music, whose flowing rhythm is broken (page 8, line 3). Characteristically descriptive of his discomfiture is the music when, in futile endeavors to clamber up to them, he inveighs against the "slippery slime" which causes him to lose his foothold (page 12, line 2).

When, after *Woglinde, Wellgunde* and *Flosshilde* have in turn gamboled almost within his reach, only to dart away again, he curses his own weakness, you hear the MOTIVE OF THE NIBELUNGS' SERVITUDE, (page 24, line 1, bars 3 and 4).

Swimming high above him the Rhinedaughters incite him with gleeful cries to chase them. *Alberich* tries to ascend, but always slips and falls back. Finally, beside himself with rage, he threatens them with clenched fist. The music accompanying this threat is in the typical rhythm of the Nibelung Motive (see No. 18).

Alberich's gaze is attracted and held by a glow which suddenly pervades the waves above him and increases until from the highest point of the central cliff a bright, golden ray shoots through the water. Amid the shimmering accompaniment of the violins is heard on the horn the RHINEGOLD MOTIVE (page 31, line 1).

With shouts of triumph the Rhinedaughters swim around the rock. Their cry, "Rhinegold," is a characteristic motive, heard again later in the cycle, and the new accompanying figure on the violins may also be noted, as later on further reference to it will be neces-

sary. THE RHINEDAUGHTERS' SHOUT OF TRIUMPH and
the accompaniment to it are as follows:

As the river glitters with golden light the Rhinegold
Motive rings out brilliantly on the trumpet. The Nibelung is fascinated by the sheen. The Rhinedaughters
gossip with one another, and *Alberich* thus learns that
the light is that of the Rhinegold, and that whoever
shapeth a ring from this gold will become invested
with great power. Then is heard THE RING MOTIVE
page 41, line 3) in the woodwind:

When *Flosshilde* bids her sisters cease their prattle,
lest some sinister foe should overhear them, the music
which accompanied *Alberich's* threat in the typical Nibelung rhythm reappears for an instant (page 42, line 3).

Wellgunde and *Woglinde* ridicule their sister's anxiety,
saying that no one would care to filch the gold, because
it would give power only to him who abjures or renounces love. The darkly prophetic MOTIVE OF THE

RENUNCIATION OF LOVE is heard here (page 43, line 1). It is sung by *Woglinde*:

7.

As *Alberich* reflects on the words of the Rhinedaughters (page 47, line 3) the Ring Motive occurs both in voice and orchestra in mysterious pianissimo (like an echo of *Alberich's* sinister thoughts), and is followed by the Motive of Renunciation.   Then is heard the sharp, decisive rhythm of the Nibelung Motive (see No. 18), and *Alberich* fiercely springs over to the central rock.   The Rhinedaughters scream and dart away in different directions.   The threatening measures of the Nibelung—this time loud and relentless—and *Alberich* has reached the summit of the highest cliff.

"Hark, ye floods!   Love I renounce forever!" he cries, and amid the crash of the Rhinegold Motive he seizes the gold and disappears in the depths.   With screams of terror the Rhinedaughters dive after the robber through the darkened water, guided by *Alberich's* shrill, mocking laugh.   Waters and rocks sink ; as they disappear, the billowy accompaniment sinks lower and lower in the orchestra.   Above it rises once more the Motive of Renunciation (page 53, line 5).   The Ring Motive is heard, and then as the waves change into nebulous clouds the billowy accompaniment rises pianissimo until, with a repetition of the Ring Motive, the action passes to the second scene.   One crime has already been committed —the theft of the Rhinegold by *Alberich*.   How that crime and the ring which he shapes from the gold inspire other crimes is told in the course of the following scenes of " Rhinegold."   Hence the significance of the

Ring Motive as a connecting link between the first and second scenes.

SCENE II.

The dawn illumines a castle with glittering turrets on a rocky height at the back. ·Through a deep valley between this and the foreground the Rhine flows.

With the opening of the second scene the stately WALHALLA MOTIVE is heard:

This is a motive of superb beauty. It greets us again and again in " Rhinegold" and frequently in the later music-dramas of the cycle. Yet, often as it occurs, one hears it with ever-growing admiration. Walhalla is the dwelling of gods and heroes and its motive is divinely and heroically beautiful. Though it is essentially broad and stately it often assumes a tender mood, like the chivalric gentleness which every true hero feels toward woman. Thus it is at the opening of the second scene, for here this motive, which when played forte or fortissimo is one of the stateliest of musical inspirations, is marked *piano* and *molto dolce*. In crescendo and decrescendo it rises and falls, as rises and falls with each breath the bosom of the beautiful *Fricka*, who slumbers at *Wotan's* side.

As *Fricka* awakens her eyes fall on the castle. In her surprise she calls to her spouse. *Wotan* dreams on, the Ring Motive, and later the Walhalla Motive, being heard in the orchestra, for with the ring *Wotan* is finally to compensate the Giants for building Walhalla. As he opens his eyes and sees the castle you hear (page 56, line 4) the "Spear Motive," which is a characteristic variation of the "Motive of Compact" (No. 9). For *Wotan* should enforce, if needful, the compacts of the Gods with his spear.

Wotan sings of the glory of Walhalla. All through his apostrophe resounds the Walhalla Motive. *Fricka* reminds him that he has made a compact with the Giants to deliver over to them for their work in building Walhalla, *Freia*, the Goddess of Youth and Beauty. This introduces on the 'cellos and double basses the MOTIVE OF COMPACT.

A theme more expressive of the binding force of law it is impossible to conceive. It has the inherent dignity and power of the idea of justice.

Then follows a little domestic spat between *Wotan* and *Fricka*, *Wotan* claiming that *Fricka* was as anxious as he to have Walhalla built, and *Fricka* answering that she desired to have it erected in order to persuade *Wotan* to lead a more domestic life. At *Fricka's* words,

"Halls, bright and gleaming,"

the FRICKA MOTIVE is heard for the first time (page 61, line 1). It is a caressing motive of much grace and beauty :

It is also prominent in *Wotan's* reply immediately following. When *Wotan* tells *Fricka* that he never intended to really give up *Freia* to the Giants, chromatics, like little tongues of fire, appear in the accompaniment (page 63, line 3). They are suggestive of the *Loge*, Motive, for with the aid of Loge, *Wotan* hopes to trick the Giants. " Then save her at once ! " calls *Fricka*, as *Freia* enters in hasty flight. At this point (page 64, line 1) is heard the first bar of the Freia Motive combined with the Flight Motive. The MOTIVE OF FLIGHT is as follows :

The following is the FREIA MOTIVE :

I give it here already in full for convenient reference. With *Freia's* exclamations that the Giants are pursuing her the first suggestion of the Giant Motive appears (page 64, line 3), and as these "great, hulking fellows" enter the heavy, clumsy GIANT MOTIVE is heard in its entirety (page 68, line 1) :

Fasolt and *Fafner* have come to demand that *Wotan* deliver up to them *Freia*, according to his promise when they agreed to build Walhalla for him. In the ensuing scene, in which *Wotan* parleys with the giants, the Giant Motive, the Walhalla Motive, the Motive of the Compact and the first bar of the Freia Motive figure until *Fasolt's* threatening words (page 72, line 1):

" Peace wane when you break your compact,"

when there is heard a version of the Motive of Compact characteristic enough to be distinguished as the MOTIVE OF COMPACT WITH THE GIANTS:

The Walhalla, Giant and Freia motives again are heard until *Fafner* speaks of the golden apples which grow in *Freia's* garden (page 74, line 1). These golden apples are the fruit of which the gods partake in order to enjoy eternal youth. The Motive of Eternal Youth, which now appears, is one of the loveliest in the Cycle. It seems as though age could not wither it, nor custom stale its infinite variety. Its first bar is reminiscent of the Ring Motive (No. 6), for there is subtle relationship between the Golden Apples of *Freia* and the Rhinegold. This is the MOTIVE OF ETERNAL YOUTH:

It is finely combined with the Giant Motive at *Fafner's* words:

" Let her forthwith be torn from them all."

Froh and *Donner*, *Freia's* brothers, enter hastily to save their sister. As *Froh* clasps her in his arms, while

Donner confronts the Giants, the Motive of Eternal Youth rings out triumphantly on the horns and wood-wind (page 75, line 4).

But *Freia's* hope is short-lived. The Motive of the Compact with the Giants, with its weighty import, resounds as *Wotan* stretches his spear between the hostile groups. For though *Wotan* desires to keep *Freia* in Walhalla, he dare not offend the Giants. But at this critical moment he sees his cunning adviser, *Loge*, approaching. These are *Loge's* characteristic motives:
Loge Motive:

Magic Fire Motive:

They are heard throughout the ensuing scene, in which *Wotan* upbraids *Loge* for not having discovered something which the Giants would be willing to accept as a

substitute for *Freia*. *Loge* says he has traveled the
world over without finding aught that would compensate man for the renunciation of a lovely woman. At
this point is heard the Motive of Renunciation. Then
follows *Loge's* narrative of his wanderings. With great
cunning he intends to tell *Wotan* of the theft of the
Rhinegold and of the wondrous worth of a ring shaped
from the gold in order to incite the listening Giants to
ask for it as a compensation for giving up *Freia*. Hence
Wagner, as *Loge* begins his narrative, has blended, with
a marvelous sense of musical beauty and dramatic fitness,
two phrases : the Freia Motive and the accompaniment to
the Rhine daughters' shout of triumph in the first scene.
Whoever will turn to page 85, line 4, last two bars of the
vocal-piano score, will find the Freia Motive in the treble
and the somewhat simplified accompaniment to the cry
" Rhinegold" in the bass. This music continues until *Loge*
says that he discovered but one (namely, *Alberich*) who
was willing to renounce love. Then the Rhinegold Motive is sounded tristly in a minor key and immediately
afterward is heard the Motive of Renunciation.

Loge next tells how *Alberich* stole the gold. All through
this portion of the narrative are heard, in the accompaniment, reminiscences of the motives of the first
scene. It should be noticed that when (page 89, line 1)
Loge gives *Wotan* the message of the Rhinedaughters,
that the chief of the gods wrest the gold from *Alberich*
and restore it to them, the Rhinegold Motive rings out
brilliantly in a major key (C major). *Loge* has already
excited the curiosity of the Giants, and when *Fafner*
asks him what power *Alberich* will gain through the
possession of the gold, he dwells upon the magical attri-
butes of the ring shaped from Rhinegold. As *Wotan*

ponders over *Loge's* words the Ring Motive is heard, for *Wotan* is planning how· he may possess himself of the ring. With true knowledge of human, and especially of feminine nature, Wagner makes *Fricka* ask if articles of jewelry could be made of the gold. As *Loge* tells her that the possession of the ring will insure *Wotan's* fidelity to her and that *Alberich's* Nibelungs are at that moment forging a ring of the Rhinegold, he sings the Fricka Motive (*Fricka* being the guardian of marriage-fidelity), while, when he refers to the Nibelungs (page 92, line 3, last two bars) there is heard for the first time the Nibelung Motive. (The Nibelung Motive will be found (No. 18) at the point when it assumes its due prominence in the score, viz., in the Nibelheim scene.) *Wotan* is evidently strongly bent on wresting the gold from *Alberich* and retaining it in his own possession instead of restoring it to the Rhinedaughters, for, as he stands wrapt in meditation (page 93, line 1), the Rhinegold Motive is heard in a minor key, and as he asks *Loge* how he may shape the gold into a ring we have the Ring Motive. *Loge* tells *Wotan* that *Alberich* has abjured love and already forged the ring. Here the Motive of Renunciation is sounded with a harsh power (page 94, line 3), expressive of *Alberich's* tyranny, which we are soon to witness.

Loge's diplomacy is beginning to bear results. *Fafner* tells *Fasolt* that he deems the possession of the gold more important than *Freia*. Notice here (page 97, line 2, last bar *et seq.*) how the Freia motive, so prominent when the Giants insisted on her as their compensation, is relegated to the bass and how (line 4, last two bars) the Rhinegold Motive breaks in upon the Motive of Eternal Youth as *Fafner* and *Fasolt* again advance toward

Wotan, for they now request *Wotan* to wrest the gold
from *Alberich* and give it to them as ransom for *Freia*.
Wotan refuses and the Giants, having proclaimed that
they will give *Wotan* until evening to determine upon
his course, seize *Freia* and drag her away. Here the
music is highly descriptive. Pallor settles upon the faces
of the gods ; they seem to have grown older. Alas, they
are already affected by the absence of *Freia*, the Goddess of Youth, whose motives are but palely reflected by
the orchestra, as *Loge*, with cunning alarm, explains the
cause of the gods' distress; until *Wotan* proclaims that
he will go with *Loge* to Nibelheim.

Loge disappears down a crevice in the side of the
rock. From it a sulphurous vapor at once issues. When
Wotan has followed *Loge* into the cleft the vapor fills the
stage and conceals the remaining characters. The va-
pors thicken to a black cloud, continually rising upward,
until rocky chasms are seen. These have an upward
motion, so that the stage appears to be sinking deeper
and deeper. During this transformation scene there is
an orchestral interlude. First is heard the Loge Motive,
four times interrupted by the Motive of Renunciation.
Beginning at page III, line 5, bar 4, the Motive of Servitude is heard during four bars. Then, with a *molto
vivace* the orchestra dashes into the Motive of Flight.
Twice the Ring and Rhinegold motives are heard, the
latter appearing the second time with the typical
Nibelung Motive (page 112, line 5), expressive of
the enslaved Nibelungs constantly working at the forge.

18.

This motive accompanies for sixteen bars, during

eight of which the rhythm is emphasized by the anvils on the stage, a broad expansion of the Flight Motive. Meanwhile from various distant quarters ruddy gleams of light illumine the chasms, and when the Flight Motive has died away, only the increasing clangor of smithies is heard from all directions. Gradually the sound of the anvils grows fainter; and, as the Ring Motive resounds like a shout of malicious triumph (expressive of *Alberich's* malignant joy at his possession of power), there is seen a subterranean cavern, apparently of illimitable depth, from which narrow shafts lead in all directions.

Scene III.

At the beginning of the third scene we hear again the measures heard when *Alberich* chased the Rhinedaughters. *Alberich* enters from a side cleft dragging after him the shrieking *Mime*. The latter lets fall a helmet which *Alberich* at once seizes. It is the tarnhelmet, made of Rhinegold, the wearing of which enables the wearer to become invisible or assume any shape. As *Alberich* closely examines the Tarnhelmet its motive is heard (page 117, line 2, beginning at the sixth bar). This is the MOTIVE OF THE TARNHELMET:

19.

To test its power *Alberich* puts it on and changes into a column of vapor. He asks *Mime* if he is visible, and when *Mime* answers in the negative *Alberich* cries out shrilly, " Then feel me instead," at the same time making poor *Mime* writhe under the blows of a visible scourge.

Alberich then departs—still in the form of a vaporous column—to announce to the Nibelungs that they are henceforth his slavish subjects. *Mime* cowers down with fear and pain. *Wotan* and *Loge* enter from one of the upper shafts. *Mime* tells them how *Alberich* has become all-powerful through the ring and the tarnhelmet made of the Rhinegold. The Motives occurring in *Mime's* narrative are the Nibelung, Servitude and Ring Motives, the latter in the terse, malignantly powerful form in which it occurred just before the opening of the third scene. Then *Alberich*, who has taken off the Tarnhelmet and hung it from his girdle, is seen in the distance, driving a crowd of Nibelungs before him from the caves below. They are laden with gold and silver, which he forces them to pile up in one place and so form a hoard. He suddenly perceives *Wotan* and *Loge*. After abusing *Mime* for permitting strangers to enter Nibelheim, he commands the Nibelungs to descend again into the caverns in search of new treasure for him, They hesitate. You hear the Ring Motive. *Alberich* draws the ring from his finger, stretches it threateningly toward the Nibelungs and commands them to obey the ring's master.

The Nibelungs disperse in headlong flight and with *Mime* rush back into the cavernous recesses. *Alberich* looks with mistrust upon *Wotan* and *Loge*. He asks them what they seek in Nibelheim. *Wotan* tells him they have heard reports of his extraordinary power and have come to ascertain if they are true. After some parleying the Nibelung points to the hoard, saying : "It is the merest heap compared to the mountain of treasure

to which it shall rise." Here appears part of the RIS-
ING HOARD MOTIVE (page 137, line 4), which in its complete form is as follows :

20.

Alberich boasts that the whole world will come under
his sway (you hear the Ring Motive), that the gods who
now laugh and love in the enjoyment of youth and
beauty will become subject to him (you hear the Freia
Motive); for he has abjured love (you hear the Motive of
Renunciation). Hence, even the gods in Walhalla shall
dread him (you hear a variation of the Walhalla Motive), and he bids them beware of the time when the
night-begotten host of the Nibelungs shall rise from
Nibelheim into the realm of daylight (you hear the
Rhinegold Motive followed by the Walhalla Motive, for
it is through the power gained by the Rhinegold that
Alberich hopes to possess himself of Walhalla). *Loge*
cunningly flatters *Alberich*, and when the latter tells him
of the Tarnhelmet feigns disbelief of *Alberich's* state-
ments. *Alberich*, to prove their truth, puts on the helmet and transforms himself into a huge serpent. The
Serpent Motive expresses the windings and writhings of
the monster.

The serpent vanishes and *Alberich* reappears. When
Loge doubts if *Alberich* can transform himself into
something very small, the Nibelung changes into a toad.
Now is *Loge's* chance. He calls to *Wotan* to set his foot
on the toad. As *Wotan* does so, *Loge* puts his hand to its
head and seizes the Tarnhelm. *Alberich* is seen writh-

ing under *Wotan's* foot. *Loge* binds *Alberich;* both seize him, drag him to the shaft from which they descended and disappear ascending. The scene now changes in the reverse direction to that in which it changed when *Wotan* and *Loge* were descending to Nibelheim. The orchestra accompanies the change of scene. The Ring Motive dies away from crashing fortissimo to piano, to be succeeded by the dark Motive of Renunciation. Then is heard the clangor of the Nibelung smithies, and amid it the Motive of Flight in its broadly-expanded form. The Giant, Walhalla, Loge and Servitude Motives follow, the last with crushing force as *Wotan* and *Loge* emerge from the cleft, dragging the pinioned *Alberich* with them. His lease of power was brief. He is again in a condition of servitude.

Scene IV.

A pale mist still veils the prospect as at the end of the second scene. *Loge* and *Wotan* place *Alberich* on the ground and *Loge* dances around the pinioned Nibelung, mockingly snapping his fingers at the prisoner. *Wotan* joins *Loge* in his mockery of *Alberich*. The Nibelung asks what he must give for his freedom. "Your hoard and your glittering gold," is *Wotan's* answer. *Alberich* assents to the ransom and *Loge* frees the gnome's right hand, *Alberich* raises the ring to his lips and murmurs a secret behest. The Nibelung Motive is heard, combined at first with the Motive of the Rising Hoard, then with the Motive of Servitude and later with both. This combination of the three Motives will be found on page 165, line 2, last bar; the Motive of Servitude being played in the right hand, the other two in the left. These three Motives continue prominent as long as the Nibelungs emerge from the cleft and heap up the hoard. Then, as *Alberich* stretches out the Ring toward them, they rush in terror toward the cleft, into which they disappear. *Alberich* now asks for his freedom, but *Loge* throws the Tarnhelmet on to the heap. *Wotan* further demands that *Alberich* also give up the ring. At these words dismay and terror are depicted on *Alberich's* face. He had hoped to save the ring, but in vain. *Wotan* tears it from the gnome's finger. Then *Alberich*, impelled by hate and rage, curses the ring. The MOTIVE OF THE CURSE is as follows :

To it should be added the syncopated measures expressive of the threatening and ever-active NIBELUNGS' HATE :

Amid the heavy thuds of the Motive of Servitude *Alberich* vanishes in the cleft.

The mist begins to rise. It grows lighter. The Giant Motive and the Motive of Eternal Youth are heard, for the giants are approaching with *Freia*. *Donner, Froh* and *Fricka* hasten to greet *Wotan*. *Fasolt* and *Fafner* enter with *Freia*. It has grown clear, except that the mist still hides the distant castle. *Freia's* presence seems to have restored youth to the gods. While the Motive of the Giant Compact resounds, *Fasolt* asks for the ransom for *Freia*. *Wotan* points to the hoard. With staves the giants measure off a space of the

height and breadth of *Freia.* That space must be filled
out with treasure.

Loge and *Froh* pile up the hoard, but the giants are
not satisfied even when the Tarnhelmet has been added.
They wish also the ring to fill out a crevice. *Wotan*
turns in anger away from them. A bluish light glimmers in the rocky cleft to the right, and through it *Erda*
rises to half her height. She warns *Wotan* against retaining possession of the ring. The Motives prominent
during the action preceding the appearance of *Erda* will
be readily recognized. They are the Giant Compact
Motive combined with the Nibelung motive (the latter
combined with the Giant Motive and Motive of the
Hoard) and the Ring Motive, which breaks in upon the
action with tragic force as *Wotan* refuses to give up the
ring to the giants. The ERDA MOTIVE bears a strong
resemblance to the Rhine Motive:

23.

The syncopated notes of the Nibelungs' malevolence,
so threateningly indicative of the harm which *Alberich*
is plotting, are also heard in *Erda's* warning (page 193,
line 4). *Wotan,* heeding her words, throws the ring
upon the hoard. The giants release *Freia,* who rushes
joyfully toward the gods. Here the Freia Motive, combined with the Flight Motive, now no longer agitated but
joyful, rings out gleefully. Soon these motives are interrupted by the Giant and Nibelung motives, there being
added to these later the Motive of the Nibelungs' Hate
and the Ring Motive. *Alberich's* curse is already beginning its dread work. The giants dispute over the
spoils, their dispute waxes to strife, and at last *Fafner*

slays *Fasolt* and snatches the ring from the dying giant. As the gods gaze horror-stricken upon the scene, the Curse Motive resounds with crushing force (page 200, line 3). *Loge* congratulates *Wotan* that he should have given up the curse-laden ring. His words are accompanied by the Motive of the Nibelungs' Hate. Yet even *Fricka's* caresses, as she asks *Wotan* to lead her into Walhalla, cannot divert the god's mind from dark thoughts, and the Curse Motive accompanies his gloomy, curse-haunted reflections.

Donner ascends to the top of a lofty rock. He gathers the mists about him until he is enveloped by a black cloud. He swings his hammer. There is a flash of lightning, a crash of thunder, and lo ! the cloud vanishes. A rainbow bridge spans the valley to Walhalla, which is illumined by the setting sun. The DONNER MOTIVE is as follows :

24.

Wotan eloquently greets Walhalla, and then, taking *Fricka* by the hand, leads the procession of the gods into the castle.

The music of this scene is of wondrous eloquence and beauty. Six harps are added to the ordinary orchestral instruments, and as the variegated bridge is seen their arpeggios shimmer like the colors of the rainbow around the broad, majestic RAINBOW MOTIVE :

25.
etc.

Then the stately Walhalla Motive resounds as the gods gaze, lost in admiration, at the Walhalla. It gives way to the Ring Motive as *Wotan* speaks of the day's ills; and then as he is inspired by the idea of begetting a race of demi-gods to conquer the Nibelungs, there is heard for the first time the SWORD MOTIVE:

But the cunning *Loge* knows that the curse must do its work, even if not until the distant future; and hence as he remains in the foreground looking after the gods, the Loge and Ring Motives are heard.

The cries of the Rhinedaughters greet *Wotan.* They beg him to restore the ring to them. But *Wotan* is deaf to their entreaties. He preferred to give the ring to the giants rather than forfeit *Freia.*

The Walhalla Motive swells to a majestic climax and the gods enter the castle. Amid shimmering arpeggios the Rainbow Motive resounds. The gods have attained the height of their glory—but the Nibelung's curse is still potent, and it will bring woe upon all who have possessed or will possess the ring until it is restored to the Rhinedaughters. *Fasolt* was only the first victim of *Alberich's* curse.

"THE VALKYR."

Wotan's enjoyment of Walhalla was destined to be short-lived. Filled with dismay by the death of *Fasolt* in the combat of the giants for the accursed Ring, and impelled by a dread presentiment that the force of the curse would be visited upon the gods, he descended from Walhalla to the abode of the all-wise woman, *Erda.* We must assume that matrimonial obligations were not strictly enforced among the gods. It may have been inferred, from *Fricka's* anxiety to have Walhalla built in order to induce *Wotan* to lead a more domestic life, that the chief god was an old offender against the marriage vow, for though *Fricka* was the guardian goddess of connubial virtue, she does not seem to have been able to hold her spouse in check. To say the least, the chief god was very promiscuous in his attentions to the gentler sex. Thus his visit to *Erda* was not entirely unremunerative, for, while he could not obtain from her a forecast of the future of the gods, she bore him nine daughters. These were the Valkyrs, headed by *Brünnhilde*—the wild horsewomen of the air, who on winged steeds bore the dead heroes to Walhalla, the warrior's heaven. With the aid of the Valkyrs and the heroes they gathered to Walhalla, *Wotan* hoped to repel any assault upon his castle by the enemies of the gods.

But though the host of heroes grew to a goodly number, the terror of *Alberich's* curse still haunted the chief of the gods. He might have freed himself from it had he returned the Ring and Helmet made of Rhinegold to the Rhinedaughters, from whom *Alberich* filched it; but in his desire to persuade the giants to relinquish *Freia*, whom he had promised to them as a reward for building Walhalla, he, having wrested the Ring from *Alberich*, gave it to the giants instead of returning it to the Rhinedaughters. He saw the giants contending for the possession of the ring and saw *Fasolt* slain—the first victim of *Alberich's* curse. He knows that the giant *Fafner*, having assumed the shape of a huge serpent, now guards the Niebelung treasure, which includes the Ring and the Tarnhelmet, in a cave in the heart of a dense forest. How shall the Rhinegold be restored to the Rhinedaughters?

Wotan hopes that this may be consummated by a human hero who, free from the lust for power which obtains among the gods shall, with a sword of *Wotan's* own forging, slay *Fafner*, gain possession of the Rhinegold and restore it to its rightful owners, thus righting *Wotan's* guilty act and freeing the gods from the curse. To accomplish this *Wotan*, in human guise as Wälse, begets in wedlock with a woman the twins *Siegmund* and *Sieglinde*. How the curse of *Alberich* is visited upon these is related in " The Valkyr."

The *dramatis personæ* in " The Valkyr " are *Brünnhilde* and her eight sister valkyrs, *Fricka, Sieglinde, Siegmund, Hunding* (the husband of *Sieglinde*), and *Wotan*. The action begins after the marriage of *Sieglinde* to *Hunding*. The earlier events in the lives of the two Wälsings we learn of in the narratives of *Siegmund* and *Wotan* respectively in the first and second acts of " The Valkyr."

Of course, the Wälsings are in ignorance of the divinity of their father. They know him only as Wälse.

ACT I.

The introduction to "The Valkyr" is very different in character from that to "The Rhinegold." In that the Rhine flowing peacefully toward the sea and the innocent gambols of the Rhinedaughters were musically depicted. But "The Valkyr" opens in storm and stress. It is as though the peace and happiness of the first scene of the cycle had vanished from the earth with *Alberich's* abjuration of love, his theft of the gold and *Wotan's* equally treacherous crime. This vorspiel is a masterly representation in tone of a storm gathering for its last infuriated onslaught. There is majestic force in its climax. The elements are unloosed. The wind sweeps through the forest. Lightning flashes in jagged streaks across the black heavens. There is a crash of thunder and the storm has spent its force.

Two leading motives are employed in this introduction. They are the STORM MOTIVE and the DONNER MOTIVE (No. 24). The STORM MOTIVE (page 1, line 1) is as follows:

27.

These themes are as elementary as that of the Fifth Symphony. From the theme of that symphony Beethoven developed a work which by many is considered his grandest. Similarly Wagner has composed, with the use of only the two motives named, the most stupendous storm music we have—not even excepting the storm of the Pastorale. I call the attention of those who still labor under the error that Wagner's methods are obscure and involved to the vorspiel to "The Valkyr."

In the early portion of this vorspiel only the string instruments are used. Gradually the instrumentation grows more powerful. With the climax we have a tremendous ff on the contra tuba and two tympani, followed by the crash of the Donner Motive on the wind instruments.

The storm then gradually dies away. Before it has quite passed over, the curtain rises, revealing the large hall of *Hunding's* dwelling. This hall is built around a huge ash-tree, whose trunk and branches pierce the roof, over which the foliage is supposed to spread. There are walls of rough-hewn boards, here and there hung with large plaited and woven hangings. In the right foreground is a large, open hearth; back of it in a recess is the larder, separated from the hall by a woven hanging, half drawn. In the background is a large door. A few steps in the left foreground lead up to the door of an inner room. The furniture of the hall is primitive and rude. It consists chiefly of a table, bench and stools in front of the ash-tree. Only the light of the fire on the hearth illumines the room; though occasionally its fitful gleam is slightly intensified by a distant flash of lightning from the departing storm.

The door in the background is opened from without. *Siegmund*, supporting himself with his hand on the bolt, stands in the entrance. He seems exhausted. His appearance is that of a fugitive who has reached the limit of his powers of endurance. Seeing no one in the hall, he staggers toward the hearth and sinks upon a bearskin rug before it, with the exclamation :

" Whose hearth this may be,
Here I must rest me."

In an Italian opera we would probably have had at this point a very amusing illustration of the total disregard for dramatic fitness which characterizes the old-fashioned opera. *Siegmund*, though supposed to be exhausted by his flight through the storm, would have had strength enough left to stand near the foot-lights and sing an aria with the regulation bravura passages, and, if he got enough applause, to sing it over again. Then only would he sink down upon the rug exhausted, but whether from singing or from his flight through the storm we would be unable to say. Wagner's treatment of this scene is masterly. As *Siegmund* stands in the entrance we hear the SIEGMUND MOTIVE (page 5, line 5):

This is a sad, weary strain on 'cellos and basses. It seems the wearier for the burden of an accompanying figure on the horns, beneath which it seems to stagger as *Siegmund* staggers toward the hearth. Thus the music not only reflects *Siegmund's* weary mien, but accompanies most graphically his weary gait. Perhaps Wagner's intention was more metaphysical. Maybe the burden beneath which the Siegmund Motive staggers is the curse of *Alberich*. It is certainly (as we shall see) through that curse that *Siegmund's* life has been one of storm and stress.

When the storm-beaten Wälsung has sunk upon the rug the Siegmund Motive is followed by the Storm Mo-

tive, *pp*—and the storm has died away. The door of
the room to the left opens and *Sieglinde* appears. She
has heard some one enter, and thinking her husband has
returned has come into the hall to meet him. Seeing a
stranger stretched upon the bearskin rug she approaches
and bends compassionately over him.

Her compassionate action is accompanied by a new
motive, which by Wagner's commentators has been entitled the Motive of Compassion. But it seems to me to
have a further meaning as expressing the sympathy between two souls, a tie so subtle that it is at first invisible
even to those whom it unites. *Siegmund* and *Sieglinde*,
it will be remembered, belong to the same race; and
though they are at this point of the action unknown to
one another, yet, as *Sieglinde* bends over the hunted,
storm-beaten *Siegmund*, that subtle sympathy causes her
to regard him with more solicitude than would be awakened by any other unfortunate stranger. Hence I have
called this motive the MOTIVE OF SYMPATHY—taking
sympathy in its double meaning of compassion and
affinity of feeling:

29.

The beauty of this brief phrase is enhanced by its un-
pretentiousness. It wells up from the orchestra as
spontaneously as pity mingled with sympathetic sorrow
wells up from the heart of a gentle woman. As it is
Siegmund who has awakened these feelings in *Sieglinde*,
the Motive of Sympathy is heard simultaneously with
the Siegmund Motive (page 7, line 4).

Siegmund, suddenly raising his head, ejaculates,
"Water, water!" *Sieglinde* hastily snatches up a drink-

ing-horn and, having quickly filled it at a spring near the house, swiftly returns and hands it to *Siegmund*. As though new hope were engendered in *Siegmund's* breast by *Sieglinde's* gentle ministration the Siegmund Motive rises higher and higher, gathering passion in its upward sweep and then, combined again with the Motive of Sympathy, sinks to an expression of heartfelt gratitude. This passage is scored entirely for strings. Yet no composer, except Wagner, has evoked from a full orchestra sounds richer or more sensuously beautiful (page 8, line 3 and 4).

Siegmund drinks, and then hands the drinking-horn back to *Sieglinde*. As his look falls upon her features he regards them with growing interest. That strange presentiment of affinity is awakened in his breast. But in him, the storm-beaten fugitive, the emotion called forth by *Sieglinde's* gentle acts is deeper than sympathy of feeling. We hear versions of the Siegmund Motive and the Motive of Flight (No. 11). But the former is no longer weary and despairing, nor the latter precipitate. It seems as though *Siegmund*, having found a haven of rest, were recalling his life's vicissitudes with that feeling of sadness

> " Which is not akin to pain,
> And resembles sorrow only
> As the mist resembles rain."

These reminiscences are followed by the LOVE MOTIVE, one of the most tenderly expressive phrases ever penned (page 9, line 3) :

30.

The melody in the entire passage (that is, in the version of the Siegmund and Flight Motives and in the

Love Motive) is played by a single 'cello, and thus is invested with a mournful beauty which seems the musical expression of the thought in the lines from Longfellow I have just quoted.

The version of the Motive of Flight preceding the Love Motive is as follows:

The Love Motive is the mainspring of this act. For this act tells the story of love from its inception to its consummation. Similarly in the course of this act the Love Motive rises by degrees of intensity from an expression of the first tender presentiment of affection to the very ecstasy of love.

Siegmund asks with whom he has found shelter. *Sieglinde* replies that the house is *Hunding's*, and she his wife, and requests *Siegmund* to await her husband's return.

> Weaponless am I:
> The wounded guest,
> He will surely give shelter,

is *Siegmund's* reply. With anxious celerity, *Sieglinde* asks him to show her his wounds. But, refreshed by the draught of cool spring water and with hope revived by her sympathetic presence, he gathers force and, raising himself to a sitting posture, exclaims that his wounds are but slight; his frame is still firm, and had sword and shield been half so firm he would not have fled from his foes. His strength was spent in flight through the storm; but the night that sank on his vision has yielded again to the sunshine of *Sieglinde's* presence. At these words the Motive of Sympathy rises like a sweet hope. *Sieglinde* fills the drinking-horn with mead and offers it to *Siegmund*. He asks her to take the first sip. She does so and then hands it to him. His eyes rest upon her while he drinks. As he returns the drinking-horn to her there are traces of deep emotion in his mien. He sighs and gloomily bows his head. The action at this point is most expressively accompanied by the orchestra. Specially noteworthy are an impassioned upward sweep of the Motive of Sympathy as *Siegmund* regards *Sieglinde* with traces of deep emotion in his mien ; the Motive of Flight as he sighs, thinking perhaps that misfortune will soon part them ; and the sad, weary Siegmund Motive as he bows his head (page 12, line 4 ; page 13, lines 1 and 2).

In a voice trembling with emotion, *Siegmund* tells her that she has harbored one whom misfortune follows whithersoever he wends his footsteps. Lest misfortune should through him enter her dwelling he will depart. With firm, determined strides he has reached the door, when *Sieglinde*, forgetting all in her growing passion, calls after him :

> Then tarry here!
> Not bringest thou woe thither
> Where sorrow already reigns.

Upon *Sieglinde*, as one of the Wälsung race, rests the curse of *Alberich*. Her words are followed by a phrase freighted with woe, the Motive of the Wälsung Race or the WÄLSUNG MOTIVE (page 15, line 1):

31.

Like the Siegmund Motive it is intoned by the 'cellos and basses.

Siegmund turns and gazes searchingly into her fea-

tures.   Sadly, and as though shamed by her outburst of
feeling, she lets her eyes sink toward the ground.   *Siegmund* returns.   He leans against the hearth.   His calm,
steady gaze rests upon her.   She slowly raises her eyes
to his.   In long silence and with deep emotion they regard each other.   In the musical accompaniment to this
scene several motives are very effectively combined.   Its
basis is appropriately formed by the Wälsung Motive.
Over this rises the Motive of Sympathy.   We then hear
the Wälsung and Flight Motives combined ; next the
Love Motive, and finally the Siegmund Motive.

Sieglinde is the first to start from the reverie.   She
hears *Hunding* leading his horse to the stall.   The
music suddenly changes in character.   Like a premo-
nition of *Hunding's* entrance we hear the HUNDING
MOTIVE, *pp*.   Then as *Hunding*, armed with spear and
shield, stands upon the threshold, this HUNDING MO-
TIVE—as dark, forbidding and portentous of woe to the
two Wälsungs as *Hunding's* sombre visage—resounds
with dread power on the tubas (page 16, line 3):

Calmly and firmly *Siegmund* meets *Hunding's* scrutiny.
Sieglinde tells her husband that she found *Siegmund*
exhausted near the hearth and refreshed him with mead.
Hunding bids her prepare the meal.   He does this with
a semblance of graciousness, and similarly his Motive
assumes a semblance of graciousness (page 17, lines 4
(last bar) and 5, and page 18, line 1).   While preparing
the meal *Sieglinde's* glance again and again wanders
over to *Siegmund. Hunding*, scanning the stranger's

features, detects in them a resemblance to those of *Sieglinde*. " How like unto her !" he mutters to himself, his words being followed by the Motive of Compact (No. 9)—for *Wotan's* surrender of the Rhinegold to the giants in order to thus fulfil his compact with them for building Walhalla necessitated the creation of the Wälsung race, through a scion of which *Wotan* hopes to see the Rhinegold restored to the Rhinedaughters.

The table is spread. The three seat themselves. *Hunding* questions *Siegmund* as to his name. *Siegmund* gazes thoughtfully before him. *Sieglinde* regards him with noticeable interest. *Hunding*, who has observed both, bids *Siegmund* gratify *Sieglinde's* curiosity, and she, little suspecting her husband's thoughts, urges *Siegmund* to tell his story. *Siegmund* in the narrative which follows conceals his identity and that of his father, evidently through fear that *Hunding* may be one of the numerous enemies of the Wälsungs. He calls himself Woeful and his father Wolf. He tells how one day in his boyhood, after hunting with his father, they returned to find their dwelling in ashes, his mother's corpse among the ruins and no trace of his twin sister. Hunted by enemies, he and his father lived a wild life in the forest until in one of the combats they were separated. In vain he sought for a trace of his father. He found only a wild wolf's fur.*

Siegmund sought to mingle with men and women, but wherever he went misfortune and strife followed him.

---

* At this point you hear the Walhalla Motive, No. 8, for the father was none other than *Wotan*, known to his human descendants, however, only as Wälse. In *Wotan's* narrative in the next act it will be found that *Wotan* purposely created these misfortunes for *Siegmund* in order to strengthen him for his task.

His last combat was in behalf of a maiden whose
brothers were forcing her to wed a man she loved not.
He defended her till shield and sword were in splinters.
Then he fled, reaching *Hunding's* house when almost
dead from exhaustion.

The story of *Siegmund* is told in melodious recitative.
It is not a melody in the old-fashioned meaning of the
term, but it fairly teems with melodiousness. It will
have been observed that incidents very different in kind
are related by *Siegmund*. It would be impossible to treat
this narrative with sufficient variety of expression in a
melody. But in Wagner's melodious recitative the musical phrases reflect every incident narrated by *Siegmund*.
For instance, when *Siegmund* tells how he went hunting
with his father there is joyous freshness and abandon
in the music, which, however, suddenly sinks to sadness as he narrates how they returned and found the
Wälsung dwelling devastated by enemies. We hear also
the Hunding Motive at this point, which thus indicates
that those who brought this misfortune upon the Wälsungs were none other than *Hunding* and his kinsmen.
As *Siegmund* tells how, when he was separated from his
father, he sought to mingle with men and women you
hear the Love Motive, while his description of his latest
combat is accompanied by the rhythm of the Hunding
Motive. Those whom *Siegmund* slew were *Hunding's*
kinsmen. Thus *Siegmund's* dark fate has driven him to
seek shelter in the house of the very man who is the
arch-enemy of his race and is bound by the laws of kin-
ship to avenge on *Siegmund* the death of kinsmen. These
are some of the salient points of *Siegmund's* narrative
concerning which much more might be written. To me
this portion of the score, whether we consider it in con-

nection with the words or as pure music, has far more value than other more popular passages, for instance, *Siegmund's* Love-song; though for some years to come probably the mass of the public will continue to regard the latter as the "gem of the opera."

As *Siegmund* concludes his narative the Wälsung Motive is heard. Gazing with ardent longing toward *Sieglinde*, he says:

> Now know'st thou, questioning wife,
> Why " Peaceful " is not my name.

These words are sung to a lovely phrase. Then, as *Siegmund* rises and strides over to the hearth while *Sieglinde*, pale and deeply affected by his tale, bows her head, there is heard on the horns, bassoons, violas and 'cellos a motive expressive of the heroic fortitude of the Wälsungs in struggling against their fate. It is the MOTIVE OF THE WÄLSUNGS' HEROISM (page 32, line 2):

It is followed by an effective variation of the Wälsung Motive, the whole concluding beautifully with the phrase last sung by *Siegmund*.

Hunding's sombre visage darkens more deeply as he rises. His were the kinsmen of the woman for whom *Siegmund* fought. The laws of hospitality make it imperative that he should give the Wälsung shelter for that night, but he bids *Siegmund* be ready for combat in the morn. He commands *Sieglinde* to prepare his night-draught. She is seen to throw spices into the horn. As she is about to enter the inner chamber she turns her eyes longingly upon the weaponless *Siegmund* and,

having attracted his attention, fixes her gaze significantly upon a spot on the trunk of the ash-tree.   As her
look falls upon the tree the SWORD MOTIVE (26) is
heard.

When *Hunding* has followed *Sieglinde, Siegmund* sinks
down upon the bearskin near the hearth and broods
over his fate.   His gloomy thoughts are accompanied
by the threatening rhythm of the Hunding Motive and
the Sword Motive *in a minor key*, for *Siegmund* is still
weaponless.   When giving vent to his thoughts, he
exclaims:

A sword my father did promise!

the Motive of Compact is heard.   But the promise appears to have been delusive and so the Compact Motive
soon loses itself in the threatening rhythm of the
Hunding Motive.   With the strength of desperation
Siegmund invokes Wälse's aid.   He cries:

Wälse! Wälse! Where is thy sword?

The Sword Motive rings out like a shout of triumph.
The embers of the fire collapse.   In the glare that for a
moment falls upon the ash-tree the hilt of a sword
whose blade is buried in the trunk of the tree is discern-
ible at the point upon which *Sieglinde's* look last rested.
While the Motive of the Sword gently rises and falls,
like the coming and going of a lovely memory, *Siegmund*
apostrophizes the sheen as the reflection of *Sieglinde's*
glance.   The embers die out.   Night falls upon the
scene.   But in *Siegmund's* thoughts the memory of that
pitying, loving look glimmers on.

The Motive of Sympathy hastening like quick footsteps—and *Sieglinde* is by *Siegmund's* side.   She has
given *Hunding* a sleeping potion.   She will point out a

weapon to *Siegmund*—a sword. If he can wield it she will call him the greatest hero, for only the mightiest can wield it. The music quickens with the subdued excitement in the breasts of the two Wälsungs. You hear the Sword Motive, and above it, on horns, clarinet and oboe, a new motive—that of the WÄLSUNGS' CALL TO VICTORY (page 44, line 1):

for *Sieglinde* hopes that with the sword the stranger, who has awakened so quickly love in her breast, will overcome *Hunding*. This motive has a resistless, onward sweep. *Sieglinde*, amid the strains of the stately Walhalla Motive, followed by the Sword Motive, narrates the story of the sword. While *Hunding* and his kinsmen were feasting in honor of her forced marriage with him, an aged stranger entered the hall. The men knew him not and shrank from his fiery glance. But upon her his look rested with tender compassion. With a mighty thrust he buried a sword up to its hilt in the trunk of the ash-tree. Whoever drew it from its sheath to him it should belong. The stranger went his way. One after another the strong men tugged at the hilt—but in vain. Then she knew who the aged stranger was and for whom the sword was destined.

The Sword Motive rings out like a joyous shout, and *Sieglinde's* voice mingles with the triumphant notes of the Wälsungs' Call to Victory as she turns to *Siegmund:*

> Oh, found I in thee
> The friend in need !

The Motive of the Wälsungs' heroism, now no longer

full of tragic import, but forceful and defiant—and *Siegmund* holds *Sieglinde* in his embrace. There is a rush of wind. The woven hangings flap and fall. As the lovers turn, a glorious sight greets their eyes. The landscape is illumined by the moon. Its silver sheen flows down the hills and quivers along the meadows whose grasses tremble in the breeze. All nature seems to be throbbing in unison with the hearts of the lovers. The voices of spring—the season when love opens like the buds—are whispered to *Siegmund* by the orchestra, and as he hears them he greets *Sieglinde* with the LOVE SONG:

35.

The Love Motive, impassioned, irresistible, sweeps through the harmonies—and Love and Spring are united. The Love Motive also pulsates through *Sieglinde's* ecstatic reply after she has given herself fully up to *Siegmund* in the Flight Motive—for before his coming her woes have fled as winter flies before the coming of spring. With *Siegmund's* exclamation:

> Oh, wondrous vision!
> Rapturous woman!

there rises from the orchestra like a vision of loveliness the Motive of Freia (No. 12), the Venus of German mythology. In its embrace it folds this pulsating theme,

B.

which throbs on like a long love-kiss until it seemingly yields to the blandishments of this caressing phrase :

This throbbing, pulsating, caressing music is succeeded by a moment of repose. While the Walhalla Motive is heard *Sieglinde* gazes searchingly into *Siegmund's* features. They are strangely familiar to her. The Love Motive weaves itself around *Siegmund's* words as he also discovers familiar traces in *Sieglinde's* mien. *Sieglinde* once saw her face reflected in the brook—it seems reflected in *Siegmund's* features. She has heard his voice —it was when she heard the echo of her own voice in the forest. His look has already gleamed upon her—it was when the stranger gazed upon her before he thrust the sword into the trunk of the ash-tree.* Was Wolf really his father—is Woeful really his name ?

Siegmund proclaims that his father was a wolf to timid foxes. But he whose glance gleamed as gleams *Sieglinde's* glance was *Wälse*. Then, while the orchestra fairly seethes with excitement, *Sieglinde*, almost beside herself, calls jubilantly to him who came to her a stranger out of the storm :

> Was Wälse thy father,
> And art thou a Wälsung !
> Thrust he for thee
> His sword in the tree !
> Then let me name thee
> As I love thee—
> Siegmund, I call thee !

---

* Notice here the combination of Sword and Wälsungs' Heroism Motives, followed by a combination of Sword and Walhalla Motives.

Siegmund leaps upon the table. The Motive of the Wälsungs' Heroism rings out in defiance of the enemies of the race. The Sword Motive—and he has grasped the hilt; the Motive of Compact, ominous of the fatality which hangs over the Wälsungs; the Motive of Renunciation, with its threatening import; then the Sword Motive—brilliant like the glitter of refulgent steel—and *Siegmund* has unsheathed the sword. The Wälsungs' Call to Victory, like a song of triumph; a superb upward sweep of the Sword Motive; the Love Motive, now rushing onward in the very ecstasy of passion, and *Siegmund* holds in his embrace *Sieglinde*—sister and bride !

ACT II.

The Vorspiel: With an upward rush of the Sword Motive, resolved into 9-8 time, the orchestra dashes into the Flight Motive. The Sword Motive in this 9-8 rhythm closely resembles the Motive of the Valkyrs' Ride (No. 37) and the Flight Motive in the version in which it appears is much like the Valkyrs' Shout (No. 36). The Ride and the Shout are heard in the course of the vorspiel, the former with tremendous force on trumpets and trombones as the curtain rises upon a wild, rocky mountain pass, at the back of which, through a natural rock-formed arch, a gorge slopes downward. In the foreground stands *Wotan*, armed with spear, shield and helmet. Before him is *Brünnhilde* in the superb costume of the Valkyrs. The stormy spirit of the Vorspiel pervades the music of *Wotan's* command to *Brünnhilde* that she bridle her steed for battle and spur it to the fray to do combat for *Siegmund* against *Hunding*.

Brünnhilde greets *Wotan's* command with the weirdly, joyous SHOUT OF THE VALKYRS:

Hojotoho! Heiaha-ha!

It is the cry of the wild horsewomen of the air, coursing through storm-clouds, their shields flashing back the lightning, their voices mingling with the shrieks of the tempest. Weirder, wilder joy has never found expression in music. The tone-colors employed by Wagner are so graphic that one sees the streaming manes of the steeds of the air and the streaks of lightning playing around their riders, and hears the whistling of the winds. It is a marvelous tone-picture, equaled only by other creations of its creator:

The accompanying figure is based on the Motive of the RIDE OF THE VALKYRS:

Brünnhilde having leapt from rock to rock, to the highest peak of the mountain, again faces *Wotan*, and with delightful banter calls to him that *Fricka* is approaching in her ram-drawn chariot. At the words:

Ha! how she wields her golden scourge,

we hear a version of the Motive of Servitude (No. 3), which occurs again when *Fricka* has appeared and descended from her chariot and advances toward *Wotan*, *Brünnhilde* having meanwhile disappeared behind the mountain height. *Wotan*, through his guilt, has become the slave of his evil conscience, and the Motive of Servitude now stands for the remorseless energy with which crime pursues its perpetrator.

The ensuing scene between *Wotan* and *Fricka* has been subjected to an immense amount of criticism and ridicule. Even Wagnerian commentators are somewhat timid in their references to it. Von Wolzogen dismisses it with a few words. It is therefore with some pride that I point to an American criticism which is justly appreciative. I refer to the letters which Mr. J. R. G. Hassard contributed from Bayreuth to the *Tribune* in 1876. The lucidity of Mr. Hassard's treatment of the subject, the felicity of his diction, his thorough comprehension of Wagner's theory and his appreciation of its artistic beauty, make these letters worthy to be ranked among the most important contributions to the musical literature of the day. This scene between *Wotan* and *Fricka* Mr. Hassard calls "another of those great dramatic scenes, full of fine discriminations, of forcible declamation, and of almost illimitable suggestiveness, which alone would point out Wagner as the greatest of writers for the musical stage."

The plain facts concerning this scene are these: It is somewhat long, and hence, from a dramatic point of view, perhaps too extended, as it delays the action. But if it may be *partially* condemned dramatically, it must be *entirely* and unreservedly praised musically. Indeed it is musically so fine that to an intelligent listener all sense of lengthiness disappears. *Fricka* is the protector of the marriage vow, and as such she has come in anger to demand from *Wotan* vengeance in behalf of *Hunding*. As she advances hastily toward *Wotan*, her angry, passionate demeanor is reflected by the orchestra, and this effective musical expression of *Fricka's* ire is often heard in the course of the scene. When near *Wotan* she moderates her pace and her angry demeanor gives way to sullen dignity. This change is also graphically depicted in the orchestra in a phrase based on the fourth bar of the *Fricka* motive (page 89, lines 2 (last bar) and 3).

Wotan feigns ignorance of the cause of *Fricka's* agitation and asks what it is that harasses her. Her reply is preceded by the stern *Hunding* motive. She tells *Wotan* that she, as the protectress of the sanctity of the marriage vow, has heard *Hunding's* voice calling for vengeance upon the Wälsung twins. Her words, " His voice for vengeance is raised," are set to a phrase strongly suggestive of *Alberich's* curse. It seems as though the avenging Nibelung were pursuing *Wotan's* children and thus striking a blow at *Wotan* himself through *Fricka*. The Love motive breathes through *Wotan's* protest that *Siegmund* and *Sieglinde* only yielded to the magic of the spring night. There is a superbly forceful strain when *Wotan* exclaims (page 91) :

> For when strong spirits are rampant
> I rouse them ever to strife.

The wrathful phrase expressive of *Fricka's* anger, heard at the beginning of the scene, introduces her invective against the nuptial union of brother and sister, which reaches a stormy climax with her exclamation :

> When was it heard of,
> That brother and sister
> Were lovers?

With the cool impudence of a *fin de siècle* husband, who is bandying words in a domestic spat, *Wotan* replies :

> Now it's been heard of!

Wotan argues that *Siegmnnd* and *Sieglinde* are

true lovers, and *Fricka* should smile instead of vent-
ing her wrath on them.   The motive of the Love
Song, the Love Motive and the caressing phrase heard
in the love scene are beautifully blended with *Wotan's*
words.   In strong contrast to these motives is the music
in *Fricka's* outburst of wrath, introduced by the phrase
reflecting her ire, which is repeated several times in the
course of this episode.   This is followed at the words,

Why mourn I thus o'er virtue and vows,

by a phrase which has a touch of pathos, for she is com-
plaining of *Wotan's* faithlessness.   When she upbraids
him for his lapses with *Erda*, the results of which were
the Valkyrs, you hear the motive of the Ride of the Valkyrs.   The passage concludes with a paroxysm of rage,
Fricka bidding *Wotan* complete his work and let the Wälsungs in their triumph trample her under their feet.   *Wotan* explains to her why he begat the Wälsung race and
the hopes he has founded upon it.   But *Fricka* mistrusts
him.   What can mortals accomplish that the gods, who
are far mightier than mortals, cannot accomplish? *Hunding* must be avenged on *Siegmund* and *Sieglinde*. *Wotan*
must withdraw his protection from *Siegmund*.   Now
appears a phrase which expresses *Wotan's* impotent
wrath—impotent because *Fricka* brings forward the un-
answerable argument that if the Wälsungs go unpun-
ished by her, as guardian of the marriage vow, she, the
Queen of the Gods, will be held up to the scorn of man-
kind.

MOTIVE OF WOTAN'S WRATH:

38.   etc.

Wotan would fain save the Wälsungs.   But *Fricka's*

argument is conclusive. He cannot protect *Siegmund*
and *Sieglinde*, because their escape from punishment
would bring degradation upon the queen-goddess and
the whole race of the gods, and result in their imme-
diate fall. *Wotan's* wrath rises at the thought of sacri-
ficing his beloved children to the vengeance of *Hunding*,
but he is impotent. His far-reaching plans are brought
to nought. He sees the hope of having the Ring restored to the Rhinedaughters by the voluntary act of a
hero of the Wälsung race vanish. The curse ot *Alberich*
hangs over him like a dark, threatening cloud.

Brünnhilde's joyous shouts are heard from the height.
Wotan exclaims that he had summoned the Valkyr to
do battle for *Siegmund*. In broad, stately measures,
Fricka proclaims that her honor shall be guarded by
Brünnhilde's shield and demands of *Wotan* an oath that
in the coming combat the *Wälsung* shall fall. *Wotan*
takes the oath and throws himself dejectedly down upon
a rocky seat. *Fricka* strides toward the back. She
pauses a moment with a gesture of queenly command before *Brünnhilde*, who has led her horse down the
height and into a cave to the right. It will be remembered that when in the beginning of this scene *Fricka*
advanced toward *Wotan* we heard a phrase expressive
of sullen dignity. The scene closes with this phrase,
but now no longer sullen. It rises in proud beauty
like a queenly woman exacting homage. This is one
of those finely artistic touches in which Wagner is
peerless.

I have purposely gone somewhat into the details of
this scene because it is still so much misunderstood.
Yet it is one of Wagner's finest conceptions, and as such
it will doubtless be universally ranked at some future

day. Aside from the contrast which *Fricka*, as the champion of virtue, affords to the forbidden revels of the spring night—a contrast of truly dramatic value— we witness the pathetic spectacle of a mighty god vainly struggling to avert ruin from his race. That it is to irresistible fate and not merely to *Fricka* that *Wotan* succumbs is made clear by the darkly ominous notes of *Alberich's* curse, which resound as *Wotan*, wrapt in gloomy brooding, leans back against the rocky seat, and also when, in a paroxysm of despair, he gives vent to his feelings, a passage which for overpowering intensity of expression stands out even from among Wagner's writings. The final words of this outburst of grief,

⌒ The saddest I among all men,

are set to this variant of the Motive of Renunciation; the meaning of this phrase having been expanded from the renunciation of love by *Alberich* to cover the renunciation of happiness which is forced upon *Wotan* by avenging fate:

Brünnhilde casts away shield, spear and helmet, and sinking down at *Wotan's* feet looks up to him with affectionate anxiety. Here we see in the Valkyr the touch of tenderness, without which a truly heroic character is never complete.

Musically it is beautifully expressed by the Love Motive, which, when *Wotan*, as if awakening from a reverie, fondly strokes her hair, goes over into the Siegmund Motive. It is over the fate of his beloved Wälsungs

Wotan has been brooding. Immediately following *Brünnhilde's* words,

What am I were I not thy will,

is a wonderfully soft yet rich melody on four horns. It is one of those beautiful details in which Wagner's works abound, yet, although these details are as numerous as they are beautiful, they seem to have escaped the attention of a good many critics. Or have these critics made an effort not to perceive them?

In *Wotan's* narrative, which now follows, the chief of the gods tells *Brünnhilde* of the events which have brought this sorrow upon him, of his failure to restore the stolen gold to the Rhinedaughters; of his dread of *Alberich's* curse; how she and her sister Valkyrs were born to him by *Erda*; of the necessity that a hero should without aid of the gods gain the Ring and Tarnhelmet from *Fafner* and restore the Rhinegold to the Rhinedaughters; how he begot the Wälsungs and inured them to hardships in the hope that one of the race would free the gods from *Alberich's* curse; of a prophecy uttered by *Erda*, that the end of the gods would be wrought if *Alberich* could win a woman as wife and beget a son; that *Alberich* had won a wife and an heir was about to be born to him.

It will have been observed that a considerable portion of *Wotan's* narrative covers some of the events which were enacted in Rhinegold. Hence a portion of the narrative is unnecessary and therefore undoubtedly faulty from a purely dramatic standpoint. It may also be not unjustly questioned if in other portions the narrative does not go into details beyond the dramatic requirements. Both the scene between *Wotan* and *Fricka* and

the narrative are too long to be given in their entirety in
a performance which begins as late as eight P. M. When,
however, Wagner's works are performed as they are at
Bayreuth, where the performances begin at four in the
afternoon and there are long intermissions during which
the listeners can saunter about the grounds surrounding
the theatre, not a note should be omitted. There cannot
be under such conditions the faintest suggestion of fa-
tigue from an undue mental strain, even on the part of
those who have become so accustomed to the insipidness
of the old-fashioned opera that they are appalled at the
mere thought—provided they retain the power of thinking—of mental effort in connection with a musico-dramatic work.

Whatever fault may be found with *Wotan's* narrative—
or rather portions of it—from a purely dramatic point of
view, it is musically most expressive from its first accents,
uttered in a choked, suppressed voice, to its eloquent
climax. The motives heard will be recognized, except
one, which is new. This is expressive of the stress to
which the gods are subjected through *Wotan's* crime.
It is first heard when *Wotan* tells of the hero who alone
can regain the ring. It is the MOTIVE OF THE GODS'
STRESS:

39.

Excited by remorse and despair *Wotan* bids farewell
to the glory of the gods. Then he in terrible mockery
blesses the Nibelung's heir. Terrified by this outburst
of wrath *Brünnhilde* asks what her duty shall be in the
approaching combat. *Wotan* commands her to do
Fricka's bidding and withdraw protection from *Sieg-*

mund. In vain *Brünnhilde* pleads for the Wälsung whom she knows *Wotan* loves, and wished a victor until *Fricka* exacted a promise from him to avenge *Hunding*. But her pleading is in vain, *Wotan* is no longer the all-powerful chief of the gods—through his breach of faith he has become the slave of fate. Hence we hear, as *Wotan* rushes away, driven by chagrin, rage and despair, chords heavy with the crushing force of fate.

Slowly and sadly *Brünnhilde* bends down for her weapons, her actions being accompanied by the Valkyr Motive. Bereft of its stormy impetuosity it is as trist as her thoughts. Lost in sad reflections, which find beautiful expression in the orchestra, she turns toward the background. Suddenly the sadly expressive phrases are interrupted by the Motive of Flight. Looking down into the valley the Valkyr perceives *Siegmund* and *Sieglinde* approaching in hasty flight. She then disappears in the cave. With magnificent crescendo the Motive of Flight reaches its climax and the two Wälsungs are seen through the natural arch. *Sieglinde* is hastening in advance of *Siegmund*. Seeking to restrain her flight, he clasps her tenderly. She stares wildly before her. Her terror of *Hunding's* pursuit has unsettled her reason. *Siegmund* speaks to her in gentle tones. Like a reminiscence of happier moments there is heard the wooing, caressing phrase of the love scene in the first act. *Sieglinde* gazes with growing rapture into *Siegmund's* eyes and throws her arms around his neck. A fiercely impassioned phrase accompanies her impetuous action. Then as her mien grows mournful we hear the sadly reflective version of the Motive of Flight which preceded the Love Motive in the first act. "Away! Away!" she shrieks, suddenly starting up from her reverie.

There is a dramatic change in the music which wildly follows her terrified ejaculations. There is noble calmness and determination in *Siegmund's* assuring words to her. They are introduced by the Motive of the Wälsung's Fortitude—that eloquent phrase, expressive of the fortitude with which the race has borne the struggle with adverse fate. Here *Siegmund* proposes to try the steel of his sword with *Hunding*. Then are heard in the distance the ominous notes of *Hunding's* horn, summoning his kinsmen to the pursuit of his wife and her lover. *Sieglinde* starts up in despair. Does not *Siegmund* hear the avenger's call, bidding the sleuth-hounds join him in the hunt for human prey? An agonizing shriek and *Sieglinde* grows suddenly rigid and stares vacantly before her, as if demented.

Eight chords of terrific force mark the climax of this scene.

In the insanity of her terror she believes that *Siegmund* is about to desert her, and with a wild cry of despair she throws herself upon his breast. A moment later she hears the distant notes of *Hunding's* horns, and starts up again in terror. She now believes that *Siegmund* has deserted her. Her agonized ejaculations, her heartrending grief—these find wonderfully vivid expression. With a furious crescendo the climax of the scene is reached, and *Sieglinde* sinks fainting into *Siegmund's* arms.

Without releasing his hold upon her, *Siegmund* lets himself down upon a rocky seat, so that when he assumes a sitting posture her head rests on his lap. Silently he gazes upon her, and then, while the Love Motive whispers of memories of bliss, he presses a kiss upon her brow.

The MOTIVE OF FATE—so full of solemn import—is now heard :

Brünnhilde, leading her horse by the bridle, appears in the entrance of the cave, and advances slowly and solemnly to the front ; then pauses and gazes upon *Siegmund.* While her earnest look rests upon him, there is heard the MOTIVE OF THE DEATH-SONG, a tristly prophetic strain :

Brünnhilde advances and then, pausing again, leans with one hand upon her charger's neck, and grasping shield and spear with the other, gazes upon *Siegmund.* Then there rises from the orchestra, in strains of rich, soft, alluring beauty, the Walhalla Motive. The Fate, Death-Song and Walhalla Motives recur, and *Siegmund,* raising his eyes and meeting *Brünnhilde's* look, questions her and receives her answers. The episode is so fraught with solemnity that the shadow of death seems to have fallen upon the scene. The solemn beauty of the music impresses itself the more upon the listener because of the agitated, agonized scene which preceded it. The alluring pleasures of Walhalla are depicted by the Walhalla Motive, beautifully blended with the Motive of the Valkyrs' Ride, as *Brünnhilde* announces that many warriors will greet *Siegmund's* coming; by the Walhalla Motive alone when she tells him that he will meet his

father in Walhalla; by the Freia Motive, borne airily upon
the buoyant Motive of the Valkyrs' Ride, as she promises
him that beauteous wish-maidens will wait upon him in
the warriors' heaven.   But these allurements are nought
to him. " Shall *Siegmund* there embrace *Sieglinde?*" he
asks; and when *Brünnhilde* answers in the negative he
spurns the delights she has held out to him.   Here he
will stand and meet *Hunding*. *Brünnhilde* tells him that
the sword upon which he relies will be shivered.   He
draws it to take *Sieglinde's* life and so pierce the fruit
of their love.   Moved to admiration by his heroic love,
Brünnhilde, in a jubilant outburst, as though a sorrow
had been lifted from her heart, proclaims that she will
give victory to *Siegmund*.

When she has disappeared the scene gradually darkens.   Heavy storm-clouds veil the crags and hide the
peak from view. *Siegmund* tenderly soliloquizes over
Sieglinde, and then kissing her gently upon the fore-
head, disappears among the clouds to meet *Hunding*.
Sieglinde gradually regains her senses.   The mountain is
now veiled in black thunder-clouds. *Hunding's* voice is
heard summoning *Siegmund* to combat.   She staggers
toward the peak.   It is suddenly illumined by lightning.
In the lurid light the combatants and *Brünnhilde* hov-
ering above *Siegmund* are seen.   As *Siegmund* aims a
deadly stroke at *Hunding* a reddish glow diffuses itself
through the clouds.   In it *Wotan* appears.   He inter-
poses his spear.   As the sword strikes it, *Siegmund's*
weapon is shattered and *Hunding* thrusts his spear into
the Wälsung's breast. *Sieglinde*, with a wild shriek,
falls to the ground. *Brünnhilde* rushes down to her, lifts
her upon her steed and urges the charger down the de-
file.   With a gesture of angry contempt *Wotan* fells

Hunding, and then, with a threat to visit upon *Brünn-hilde* dire punishment for her revolt against his will, he disappears amid lightning and thunder. It is impossible in words to do justice to the savage beauty of this clos-ing scene. The music is of the most dramatic charac-ter. The warring elements seem to add to the terror of this battle among the clouds. Amid these dark scenes *Alberich's* second victim finds his death.

Act III.

The third act opens with the famous ride of the Valkyrs, a number so familiar that detailed reference to it is scarcely necessary. The wild maidens of Walhalla coursing upon winged steeds through storm-clouds, their weapons flashing in the gleam of lightning, their weird laughter mingling with the crash of thunder as they bear slain warriors to the hero's heaven—such is the episode Wagner has depicted with marvelous art. The climax of barbaric joy is reached when the voices of six of the sisters unite in the shout, Hojotoho! Heiha! When eight of the Valkyrs have gathered upon the rocky summit of the mountain, which is their trysting-place, they see *Brünnhilde* approaching.

The Motive of the Gods' Stress is the chief theme heard in the ensuing scene when *Brünnhilde* tells of her disobedience to *Wotan* and begs the Valkyrs aid her to shield *Sieglinde.*

The latter, who has been lost in gloomy brooding, starts at her rescuer's supplication and in strains replete with mournful beauty begs that she may be left to her fate and follow *Siegmund* in death. The glorious prophecy of *Brünnhilde*, in which she now foretells the

birth of *Siegfried* to *Sieglinde*, is based upon the SIEG-
FRIED MOTIVE.

Sieglinde in joyous frenzy blesses *Brünnhilde* and
hastens to find safety in a dense forest to the eastward,
the same forest in which *Fafner*, in the form of a serpent, guards the Rhinegold treasures.

Wotan, in hot pursuit of *Brünnhilde*, reaches the
mountain summit.   In vain her sisters entreat him to
spare her.   He harshly threatens them unless they cease
their entreaties, and with wild cries of fear they hastily
depart.   In the ensuing scene between *Wotan* and
Brünnhilde, in which the latter seeks to justify her
action, is heard one of the most beautiful themes of the
cycle.

It is the MOTIVE OF BRÜNNHILDE'S PLEADING, which
finds its loveliest expression when she addresses *Wotan*
in the passage beginning:

Thou, who this love within my breast inspired.

In the scene there are many passages of rare beauty
and many climaxes of great dramatic power.   The principal motives employed therein the listener will readily

recognize, so that it is only necessary to give in notation
the SLUMBER MOTIVE:

This great scene between *Wotan* and *Brünnhilde*
is introduced by an orchestral passage. The Valkyr lies
in penitence at her father's feet. In the expressive orchestral measures the Motive of Wotan's Wrath mingles
with that of Brünnhilde's Pleading. The motives thus
form a prelude to the scene in which the Valkyr seeks
to appease her father's anger, not through a specious
plea, but by laying bare the promptings of a noble
heart, which forced her, against the chief god's command, to intervene for *Siegmund.* The Motive of Brünnhilde's Pleading is heard in its simplest form at *Brünnhilde's* words :

Was it so shameful what I have done,

and it may be noticed that as she proceeds the Motive
of Wotan's Wrath, heard in the accompaniment, grows
less stern until with her plea,

Soften thy wrath,

it assumes a tone of regretful sorrow.

Wotan's feelings toward *Brünnhilde* have softened for
the time from anger to grief that he must mete out punishment for her disobedience. In his reply excitement
subsides to gloom. It would be difficult to point to
other music more touchingly expressive of deep con-
trition than the phrase in which *Brünnhilde* pleads that
Wotan himself taught her to love *Siegmund.* It is here

that the Motive of Brünnhilde's Pleading assumes the
form in the notation given above. Then we hear from
Wotan that he had abandoned *Siegmund* to his fate, because he had lost hope in the cause of the gods and
wished to end his woe in the wreck of the world. The
weird terror of the Curse Motive hangs over this outburst of despair. In broad and beautiful strains *Wotan*
then depicts *Brünnhilde* blissfully yielding to her emotions when she intervened for *Siegmund*.

At last *Brünnhilde* seeks, with the prophecy of *Siegfried*, to move *Wotan* from his purpose, which is to
punish her by causing her to fall into a deep sleep and
thus become the prey of man. The motive of her pleading, reaching a magnificent climax, passes over to the
stately Siegfried Motive as she prays *Wotan* to surround
her sleeping form with horrors which only a true hero
will dare strive to overcome. Let him conjure up fire
'round about her! *Wotan* raises her to her feet and
gazes, overcome with deep emotion, into her eyes. After
a majestic orchestral passage there begins *Wotan's* farewell to *Brünnhilde*, which in all musico-dramatic num-
bers for bass voice has no peer. Such tender, mournful beauty has never found expression in music—and
this, whether we regard the vocal part or the orchestral
accompaniment in which the Slumber Motive quoted
above is prominent. *Wotan* gently leads *Brünnhilde* to
a table rock, upon which she sinks. He closes her helmet and covers her with her shield. Then, pointing his
spear toward a huge rock, he invokes *Loge*. Tongues of
fire leap up from crevices in the rocks. Flickering
flames break out on all sides. The forest glows with
fire. The magic conflagration—wildly fluttering flames
—surrounds *Wotan* and *Brünnhilde*. He gazes fondly

upon her form and then vanishes among the flames. The Slumber Motive, the Magic Fire Motive and the Siegfried Motive combine to place the music of this scene with the most brilliant and beautiful portion of our heritage from the master-musician. Toward the close of this glorious finale we hear again the ominous muttering of the Motive of Fate. *Brünnhilde* may be saved from ignominy, *Siegfried* may be born to *Sieglinde*—but the crushing weight of the hand of fate rests upon the race of the gods.

"SIEGFRIED."

The Nibelungs were not present in the dramatic action of "The Valkyr," though the sinister influence of *Alberich* shaped the tragedy of *Siegmund's* death. In "Siegfried" several characters of "The Rhinegold," who do not take part in "The Valkyr," reappear. These are the Nibelungs *Alberich* and *Mime*; the giant *Fafner*, who in the guise of a serpent guards the ring, the tarn-helmet and the Nibelung hoard in a cavern, and *Erda*. *Siegfried* has been born of *Sieglinde*, who died in giving birth to him. This scion of the Wälsung race has been reared by *Mime*, who is plotting to obtain possession of *Fafner's* treasures, and hopes to be aided in his designs by the lusty youth. *Wotan*, disguised as a wanderer, is watching the course of events, again hopeful that a hero of the Wälsung race will free the gods from *Alberich's* curse. Surrounded by magic fire, *Brünnhilde* still lies in deep slumber on the rock of the Valkyrs.

The vorspiel of "Siegfried" is expressive of *Mime's* planning and plotting. It begins with music of a mysterious, brooding character. Mingling with this is the Motive of the Hoard (No. 20), familiar from "The Rhinegold." Then is heard the Nibelung Motive (No. 18), and later, joined with it, the Motive of the Nibelung's Servitude (No. 3). After reaching a forceful climax the Motive of the Nibelung passes over to the Motive of the Ring (No. 6), which rises from pianissimo to a crash of tremendous power. The ring is to be the prize of all *Mime's* plotting, when *Siegfried*, with a sword of *Mime's* forging, shall have slain *Fafner*. The felicitous use of the Sword Motive toward the close of the vorspiel will be readily recognized, as well as the aptness of the Nibelung and Servitude Motives as expressive of *Mime's* slavish labors, and gaining further point when joined by the Dragon or SERPENT Motive.

The three motives last named are prominent in the opening scene, which shows *Mime* forging a sword at a natural forge formed in a rocky cave. In a soliloquy he discloses the purpose of his labors and laments that *Siegfried* shivers every sword which has been forged for him. Could he (*Mime*) but unite the pieces of *Siegmund's* sword ! At this thought the Sword Motive rings out brilliantly, and is jubilantly repeated, accompanied by a variant of the Walhalla Motive. For if the pieces of the sword were welded together, and *Siegfried* were with it to slay *Fafner*, *Mime* could surreptitiously obtain possession of the ring, slay *Siegfried*, rule over the gods in Walhalla and circumvent *Alberich's* plans for regaining the hoard. This last aspect of *Mime's* plan is musically expressed by the mocking phrase heard when in "The Rhinegold" *Wotan* and *Loge* made sport over the pinioned *Alberich*. This passage will be found on pages 8 and 9 of the Kleinmichel piano-score with words, beginning at bar 16 of the former and ending at 3 of the latter. The nine bars are an admirable example of the wealth of meaning in Wagner's music-drama scores, a meaning perfectly intelligible to anyone who approaches the subject in a serious, studious mood.

Mime is still at work when *Siegfried* enters, clad in a wild forest garb. Over it a silver horn is slung by a chain. The sturdy youth has captured a bear. He leads it by a bast rope, with which he gives it full play, so that it can make a dash at *Mime*. As the latter flees terrified behind the forge, *Siegfried* gives vent to his high spirits in shouts of laughter. Musically his buoyant nature is expressed by a theme inspired by the fresh, joyful spirit of a wild, woodland life. It may be called, to distinguish it from the Siegfried Motive, the MOTIVE OF SIEGFRIED THE FEARLESS.

It pervades with its joyous impetuosity the ensuing scene, in which *Siegfried* has his sport with *Mime*, until tiring of it, he loosens the rope from the bear's neck and drives the animal back into the forest. In a pretty, graceful phrase *Siegfried* tells how he blew his horn, hoping it would be answered by a pleasanter companion than *Mime*. Then he examines the sword which *Mime* has been forging. The Siegfried Motive resounds as he inveighs against the weapon's weakness, until, as he shivers the sword on the anvil, the orchestra with a rush takes up the MOTIVE OF SIEGFRIED THE IMPETUOUS.

This is a theme full of youthful snap and dash. It alternates effectively with a contraction of the Nibelung

Smithy Motive, while *Siegfried* angrily scolds *Mime* and
the latter protests. Finally *Mime* tells *Siegfried* how he
tenderly reared him from infancy. The music here is
as simple and pretty as a folk-song, for *Mime's* reminiscences of *Siegfried's* infancy are set to a charming
melody, as though *Mime* were recalling to *Siegfried's*
memory a cradle song of those days. But *Siegfried*
grows impatient. If *Mime* tended him so kindly, why
should *Mime* be so repulsive to him; and yet why
should he, in spite of *Mime's* repulsiveness, always return
to the cave? The dwarf explains that he is to *Siegfried*
what the father is to the fledgling. This leads to a beautiful lyric episode. *Siegfried* says that he saw the birds
mating, the deer pairing, the she-wolf nursing her cubs.
Whom shall *he* call *Mother?* Who is *Mime's* wife? This
episode is pervaded by a lovely, tender motive—the Mo-
TIVE OF LOVE-LIFE:

47.

Mime endeavors to persuade *Siegfried* that he is his
father and mother in one. But *Siegfried* has noticed

that the young of birds and deer and wolves look like
the parents. He has seen his features reflected in the
brook and knows he does not resemble the hideous
Mime. The notes of the Love-Life Motive pervade like
woodland strains the musical accompaniment of this
episode, in which, when *Siegfried* speaks of seeing his
own likeness, we also hear the Siegfried Motive. The
scene which follows is full of mournful beauty. *Mime*,
forced by *Siegfried* to speak the truth, tells of *Sieglinde's*
death while giving birth to *Siegfried.* Throughout this
scene we find reminiscences of the first act of "The
Valkyr," the Wälsung Motive, Motive of Sympathy and
Love Motive. Finally, when *Mime* produces as evidence
of the truth of his words the two pieces of *Siegmund's*
sword, the Sword Motive rings out brilliantly. *Siegfried*
exclaims that *Mime* must weld the pieces into a trusty
weapon. Here (page 44, line 1) the Motive of Siegfried
the Fearless assumes the form in which it is quoted
on page 66. The Motive of Siegfried the Impetuous
breaks in upon it and the Sword Motive throws its lustre
over the music. Then follows Siegfried's Wander Song, so
full of joyous abandon. Once the sword welded, he will
leave the hated *Mime* forever. As the fish darts through
the water, as the bird flies so free, he will flee from the
repulsive dwarf. With joyous exclamations he runs from
the cave into the forest.

In the scenes of which I have just spoken, the frank,
boisterous nature of *Siegfried* is charmingly portrayed.
His buoyant vivacity finds capital expression in the
Motives of Siegfried the Fearless, Siegfried the Impetuous and his Wander Song, while the vein of tenderness in his character seems to run through the Love-Life
Motive. His harsh treatment of *Mime* is not brutal ; for

Siegfried frankly avows his loathing of the dwarf, and we feel, knowing *Mime's* plotting against the young Wälsung, that *Siegfried's* hatred is the spontaneous aversion of a frank nature for an insidious one.

After *Siegfried* has disappeared in the forest, there is a gloomy soliloquy for *Mime*, interrupted by the entrance of *Wotan*, disguised as a wanderer. The ensuing scene is one of those lapses from dramatic effectiveness which we find in Wagner, and which surprise us so much, because Wagner was really an inspired dramatist, his works being constructed on fine dramatic lines, the action worked up to fine climaxes and the characters drawn in bold, broad strokes. But occasionally he has committed the error against the laws of dramatic construction of unduly prolonging a scene and thus retarding the dramatic action.

The scene between the *Wanderer* and *Mime* covers twenty-seven pages in the Kleinmichel piano-score with words, yet it advances us only one step in the dramatic action. As the *Wanderer* enters, *Mime* is in despair because he cannot weld the pieces of *Siegmund's* sword. When the *Wanderer* departs, he has prophesied that only he who does not know what fear is can weld the fragments, and that through this fearless hero *Mime* shall lose his life. This prophecy is reached through a somewhat curious process, which must be unintelligible to anyone who has not made a study of the libretto. The *Wanderer*, seating himself, wagers his head that he can correctly answer any three questions which *Mime* may put to him. *Mime* then asks: What is the race born in the earth's deep bowels? The *Wanderer* answers: The Nibelungs. *Mime's* second question is: What race dwells on the earth's back? The *Wanderer* replies:

The race of the giants. *Mime* finally asks : What race dwells on cloudy heights? The *Wanderer* answers : The race of the gods. The *Wanderer,* having thus answered correctly *Mime's* three questions, now puts three questions to *Mime:* "What is that noble race which *Wotan* ruthlessly dealt with, and yet which he deemeth most dear?" *Mime* answers correctly: "The Wälsungs." Then the *Wanderer* asks: "What sword must *Siegfried* then strike with, dealing to *Fafner* death?" *Mime* answers correctly: "With *Siegmund's* sword." "Who," asks the *Wanderer,* "can weld its fragments?" *Mime* is terrified, for he cannot answer. Then *Wotan* utters the prophecy of the fearless hero. Whoever will read over this scene will observe that in *Wotan's* answers the story of "The Rhinegold" is partially retold, and that in *Mime's* answers we have a rehearsal of "The Valkyr." Of course the narrative repetitions of the plots of preceding music - dramas are undramatic. But I have an idea that Wagner, conjecturing that in many opera - houses his tetralogy would not be given as a whole, and that in some only one or two of the four music-dramas constituting it would be played, purposely introduced these narrative repetitions in order to familiarize the audience with what preceded the particular music-drama.

But if the scene is dramatically defective, it is musically most eloquent. It is introduced by two motives, representing *Wotan* as the *Wanderer.* The mysterious chords of the former seem characteristic of WOTAN'S DISGUISE.

48.

The latter, with its plodding, heavily-tramping movement, is the MOTIVE OF WOTAN'S WANDERING.

The third new motive found in this scene is characteristically expressive of the CRINGING MIME.

Several familiar motives from "The Rhinegold" and "The Valkyr" are heard here. The Motive of Compact (No. 9), so powerfully expressive of the binding force of law, the Nibelung (No. 18), Giants' (No. 13) and Walhalla (No. 8) motives from "The Rhinegold," and the Wälsungs' Heroism motives from the first act of "The Valkyr," are among these.

When the *Wanderer* has vanished in the forest *Mime* sinks back on his stool in despair. Staring after *Wotan* into the sunlit forest, the shimmering rays flitting over the soft green mosses with every movement of the branches and each tremor of the leaves seem to him like flickering flames and treacherous will-o'-the-wisps. We hear the Loge Motive (*Loge* being the god of fire) familiar from "The Rhinegold" and the finale of "The Valkyr." At last *Mime* rises to his feet in terror. He seems to see *Fafner* in his serpent's guise appoaching to devour him, and in a paroxysm of fear he falls with a shriek behind the anvil. Just then *Siegfried* bursts out of the thicket, and with the fresh, buoyant Wander-song and the Motive of Siegfried the Fearless, the weird mystery which hung over the former scene is dispelled. *Siegfried* looks about him for *Mime* until he sees the dwarf lying behind the anvil.

Laughingly the young Wälsung asks the dwarf if he has thus been welding the sword. " The sword? The sword?" repeats *Mime*, confusedly, as he advances, and his mind wanders back to *Wotan's* prophecy of the fearless hero. Regaining his senses, he tells *Siegfried* there is one thing he has yet to learn, namely, to be afraid ; that his mother charged him (*Mime*) to teach fear to him (*Siegfried*). At this point there is heard a combination of the Wälsung Motive and the Nibelung Motive in its contracted form as it previously occurs in this act. *Mime* asks *Siegfried* if he has never felt his heart beating when in the gloaming he heard strange sounds and saw weirdly glimmering lights in the forest. *Siegfried* replies that he never has. He knows not what fear is. If it is necessary before he goes forth in quest of adventure to learn what fear is he would like to be taught. But how can *Mime* teach him?

The Magic Fire Motive and Brünnhilde's Slumber Motive, familiar from Wotan's Farewell, and the Magic Fire scene in the third act of "The Valkyr" are heard here, the former depicting the weirdly glimmering lights with which *Mime* has sought to infuse dread into *Siegfried's* breast, the latter prophesying that, penetrating fearlessly the fiery circle, *Siegfried* will reach *Brünnhilde*. Then *Mime* tells *Siegfried* of *Fafner*, thinking thus to strike terror into the young Wälsung's breast. But far from it! *Siegfried* is incited by *Mime's* words to meet *Fafner* in combat. Has *Mime* welded the fragments of *Siegmund's* sword, asks *Siegfried*. The dwarf confesses his impotency. *Siegfried* seizes the fragments.

He will forge his own sword. Here begins the great scene of the forging of the sword. Like a shout of victory the Motive of Siegfried the Fearless rings out and the orchestra fairly glows as *Siegfried* heaps a great mass of coal on the forge-hearth, and, fanning the heat, begins to file away at the fragments of the sword.

The roar of the fire, the sudden intensity of the fierce white heat to which the young Wälsung fans the glow—these we would respectively hear and see were the music given without scenery or action, so graphic is Wagner's score. The Sword Motive leaps like a brilliant tongue of fire over the heavy thuds of a forceful variant of the Motive of Compact, till brightly gleaming runs add to the brilliancy of the score, which reflects all the quickening, quivering effulgence of the scene. How the music flows like a fiery flood and how it hisses as *Siegfried* pours the molten contents of the crucible into a mold and then plunges the latter into water! The glowing steel lies on the anvil and *Siegfried* swings the hammer. With every stroke his joyous excitement is intensified. At last the work is done. He brandishes the sword and with one stroke cleaves the anvil from top to bottom. With the crash of the Sword Motive, united with the Motive of Siegfried the Fearless, the orchestra dashes into a furious prestissimo, and *Siegfried*, shouting with glee, holds his sword aloft.

ACT II.

The second act opens with a darkly portentous vorspiel. On the very threshold of it we meet *Fafner* in his motive, which is so clearly based on the Giant Motive that there is no necessity for quoting it. Through themes which are familiar from earlier por-

tions of the work, the vorspiel rises to a crashing fortissimo.   The curtain lifts on a thick forest.   At the back
is the entrance to *Fafner's* cave, the lower part of which
is hidden by rising ground in the middle of the stage,
which slopes down toward the back.   In the darkness
the outlines of a figure are dimly discerned.   It is the
Nibelung *Alberich*, haunting the domain which hides
the treasures of which he was despoiled.   The Motive of
the Nibelung's Malevolence accompanies his malicious
utterances.   From the forest comes a gust of wind.   A
bluish light gleams from the same direction.   *Wotan*,
still in the guise of a wanderer, enters.

The ensuing scene between *Alberich* and the *Wanderer*
is, from a dramatic point of view, episodical.   For this
and the further reason that the reader will readily
recognize the motives occurring in it, detailed con-
sideration of it is unnecessary.   Suffice it to say that
the fine self-poise of *Wotan* and the maliciously restless
character of *Alberich* are superbly contrasted.   When
Wotan has departed the Nibelung slips into a rocky
crevice, where he remained hidden when *Siegfried* and
Mime enter.   *Mime* endeavors to awaken dread in
Siegfried's heart by describing *Fafner's* terrible form
and powers.   But *Siegfried's* courage is not weakened.
On the contrary, with heroic impetuosity, he asks to be
at once confronted with *Fafner*.   *Mime*, well knowing
that *Fafner* will soon awaken and issue from his cave
to meet *Siegfried* in mortal combat, lingers on in the
hope that both may fall, until the young Wälsung drives
him away.

Now begins the most beautiful lyric episode ever
conceived.   *Siegfried* reclines under a linden tree, and
looks up through the branches.   The rustling of the

trees is heard. Over the tremulous whispers of the orchestra—known from concert programs as the Waldweben (forest-weaving)—rises a lovely variant of the Wälsung Motive. *Siegfried* is asking himself how his mother may have looked, and this variant of the theme which was first heard in " The Valkyr," when *Sieglinde* told *Siegmund* that her home was the home of woe, rises like a memory of her image. Serenely the sweet strains of the Love-Life Motive soothe his sad thoughts. The graceful outlines of the Freia Motive rise for a moment, and then *Siegfried*, once more entranced by forest sounds, listens intently. Birds' voices greet him. A little feathery songster, whose notes mingle with the rustling leaves of the linden tree, especially charms him.

The forest voices—the humming of insects, the piping of the birds, the amorous quiver of the branches—quicken his half-defined aspirations. Can the little singer explain his longing? He listens, but cannot catch the meaning of the song. Perhaps, if he can imitate it, he may understand it. Springing to a stream hard by, he cuts a reed with his sword, and quickly fashions a pipe from it. He blows on it, but it sounds shrill. He listens again to the bird. He may not be able to imitate its song on the reed, but on his silver horn he can wind a woodland tune. Putting the horn to his lips he makes the forest ring with its notes.*

The notes of the horn have awakened *Fafner*, who now crawls toward *Siegfried*. Perhaps the less said about the combat between *Siegfried* and *Fafner* the better. This scene, which seems very spirited in the libretto,

---

* The Motives are the Motive of Siegfried the Fearless and the Siegfried Motive.

is ridiculous on the stage. To make it effective it should be carried out very far back—best of all out of sight—so that the magnificent music will not be marred by the sight of an impossible monstrum. The music is highly dramatic. The exultant force of the Motive of Siegmund the Fearless, which rings out like a shout of barbaric joy as *Siegfried* rushes upon *Fafner*, the crashing chord as the serpent roars when *Siegfried* buries the sword in its heart, the rearing, plunging music as the monster rears and plunges with agony—these are some of the most graphic features of the score.*

Siegfried raises his fingers to his lips and licks the blood from them. Immediately after the blood has touched his lips he seems to understand the bird, which has again begun its song, while the forest voices once more weave their tremulous melody. The bird tells *Siegfried* of the ring and helmet and of the other treasures in *Fafner's* cave, and *Siegfried* enters it in quest of them. With his disappearance the forest-weaving suddenly changes to the harsh, scolding notes heard in the beginning of the Nibelheim scene in the "The Rhinegold." *Mime* slinks in and timidly looks about him to make sure of *Fafner's* death. At the same time *Alberich* issues forth from the crevice in which he was concealed. This scene, in which the two Nibelungs berate each other after the liveliest fashion, is episodical, being hardly necessary to the development of the plot. It is, however, capitally treated, and its humor affords a striking contrast to the preceding scenes.**

As *Siegfried* comes out of the cave and brings the ring

---

* Observe the significant occurrence of the Motives of the Curse, Siegfried and the Nibelungs' Malevolence in the accompaniment to *Fafner's* dying words.

** The Nibelung and Tarnhelmet Motives are prominent.

and helmet from darkness to the light of day there are heard the Ring Motive, the Motive of the Rhinedaughters' Shout of Triumph and the Rhinegold Motive.

These, familiar from " Rhinegold," will be found quoted in the analysis of it. The forest-weaving again begins, and the bird bids the young Wälsung beware of *Mime.* The dwarf now approaches *Siegfried* with repulsive sycophancy. But under a smiling face lurks a plotting heart. *Siegfried* is enabled through the supernatural gifts with which he has become endowed to fathom the purpose of the dwarf, who, unconsciously discloses his scheme to poison *Siegfried.* The young Wälsung slays *Mime,* who, as he dies, hears *Alberich's* mocking laugh. *Alberich* has felled another victim. Though the Motive of Siegfried the Fearless predominates at this point, we also hear the Nibelung Motive and the Motive of the Curse—indicating the Nibelung's evil intent toward *Siegfried.*

Siegfried again reclines under the linden. His soul is tremulous with an undefined longing. As he gazes in almost painful emotion up to the branches and asks if the bird can tell him where he can find a friend, his being seems stirred by awakening passion.

The music quickens with an impetuous phrase (p. 228, l. 3), which seems to define the first joyous thrill of passion in the youthful hero. It is the Motive of LOVE'S JOY (51).

It is interrupted (p. 229, l. 2,) by a beautiful variant of the Motive of Love-life (No. 47), which continues until above the Forest-weaving the bird again thrills him with its tale of the glorious maid who has so long slumbered upon the fire-guarded rock. With the Motive of Love's Joy coursing through the orchestra, *Siegfried*, bids the feathery songster continue, and, finally, to guide him to *Brünnhilde.* In answer, the bird flutters from the linden branch, hovers

over *Siegfried*, and hesitatingly flies before him until it
takes a definite course toward the background. *Siegfried*

51

follows the little singer, the Motive of Love's Joy, succeeded by that of Siegfried the Fearless, bringing the act
to a close.

ACT III.

The third act opens with a stormy introduction, in which
the Motive of the Ride of the Valkyrs accompanies the
Motive of the Gods' Stress (p. 239, l. 4, bar 3), the Compact and the Erda Motives (p. 239, l. 6, bar 3). The introduction reaches its climax with the MOTIVE OF THE DUSK
OF THE GODS (No. 52 *infra*).

Then to the sombre, questioning phrase of the Motive of
Fate, the action begins to disclose the significance of this
vorspiel. A wild region at the foot of a rocky mountain is
seen. It is night. A fierce storm rages. In dire stress
and fearful that through *Siegfried* and *Brünnhilde* the

rulership of the world may pass from the gods to the human race, *Wotan* summons *Erda* from her subterranean dwelling. But *Erda* has no counsel for the storm-driven, conscience-stricken god. The chief motives which accompany the scene up to this point are familiar from earlier portions of the Cycle. They are, besides the Erda and Compact Motives, the Motive of the Dusk of the Gods (p. 244, l. 3,

52

bar 7), the Walhalla and Fate Motives, and those of the Renunciation, and Brünnhilde's Pleading.

The scene reaches its climax in *Wotan's* noble renunciation of the empire of the world. Weary of strife, weary of struggling against the decree of fate he renounces his sway. Let the era of human love supplan this dynasty, sweeping away the gods and the Nibelungs in its mighty current. For mournful dignity this episode is unrivalled. It is the last defiance of all-conquering fate by the ruler of a mighty

race.   After a powerful struggle against irresistible forces,
Wotan comprehends that the twilight of the gods will be
the dawn of a more glorious epoch.   A phrase of great
dignity gives force to   *Wotan's* utterances.   It is the
MOTIVE OF THE WORLD'S HERITAGE:

53

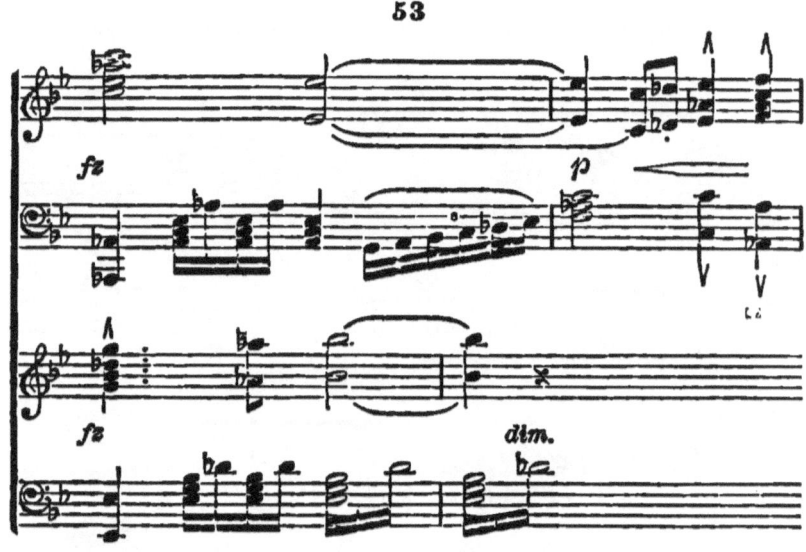

Siegfried enters, guided to the spot by the bird ; *Wotan*
checks his progress with the same spear which shivered
Siegmund's sword.   *Siegfried* must fight his way to
Brünnhilde.   With a mighty blow the young Wälsung
shatters the spear and *Wotan* disappears 'mid the crash
of the Motive of Compact—for the spear with which it was
the chief god's duty to enforce compacts is shattered.
Meanwhile the gleam of fire has become noticeable.   Fiery
clouds float down from the mountain.   *Siegfried* stands at
the rim of the magic circle.   Winding his horn he plunges
into the seething flames.   Around the Motive of Siegfried
the Fearless and the Siegfried Motive flash the Magic

Fire and Loge Motives. On p. 282, l. 3, bar 1 the Rhine-daughters' Shout of Triumph (No. 5) will be found combined with the Motive of Siegfried the Fearless and—beginning p. 284, l. 5, bar 3—there is an interesting sequence of the Siegfried Motive and the Rhine-daughters' Shout of Triumph combined with the Slumber Motive. *Siegfried* is seen ascending the heights.

The flames having flashed forth with dazzling brilliancy gradually pale before the red glow of dawn till a rosy mist envelopes the scene. When it rises, the Valkyr's Rock and *Brünnhilde* in deep slumber under the fir tree, as in the finale of " The Valkyr," are seen. *Siegfried* appears on the height in the background. As he gazes upon the scene there are heard the Fate and Slumber Motives and then the orchestra weaves a lovely variant of the Freia Motive (No. 12). This is followed by the softly caressing strains of the Fricka Motive (No. 10). *Fricka* sought to make *Wotan* faithful to her by bonds of love, and hence the Fricka Motive in this scene does not reflect her personality but rather the awakening of the love which is to thrill *Siegfried* when he has beheld *Brünnhilde's* features. As he sees *Brünnhilde's* charger slumbering in the grove we hear the Motive of the Valkyrs' Ride and, when his gaze is attracted by the sheen of *Brünnhilde's* armor, the theme of Wotan's Farewell (p. 62, *sup.*). Approaching the armed slumberer under the fir tree *Siegfried* raises the shield and discloses the figure of the sleeper, the face being almost hidden by the helmet.

He carefully loosens the helmet. As he takes it off *Brünnhilde's* face is disclosed and her long curls flow down over her bosom. *Siegfried* gazes upon her enraptured. Drawing his sword he cuts through the rings of mail on both sides, gently lifts off the corselet and greaves, and

Brünnhilde, in soft female drapery, lies before him. He starts back in wonder. Notes of impassioned import—the Motive of Love's Joy—express the feelings that well up from his heart as for the first time he beholds a woman. The fearless hero is infused with fear by a slumbering woman. The Wälsung Motive, afterwards beautifully varied with the Motive of Love's Joy, accompanies his

54

utterances, the climax of his emotional excitement being expressed in a majestic *crescendo* of the Freia Motive (p. 294, l. 4, bar 4, *et seq.*). A sudden feeling of awe gives him at least the outward appearance of calmness. With the Motive of Fate he faces his destiny; and then, while the Freia Motive rises like a vision of loveliness, he sinks over *Brünnhilde*, and with closed eyes presses his lips to hers.

Brünnhilde awakens. *Siegfried* starts up. She rises

and with noble gesture greets in majestic accents her return to the sight of earth. Strains of loftier eloquence than those of her greeting have never been composed. *Brünnhilde* rises from her magic slumbers in the majesty of womanhood (No. 54 *supra*).

With the Motive of Fate she asks who is the hero who has awakened her. The superb Siegfried Motive gives back the proud answer. In rapturous phrases they greet one another. It is the MOTIVE OF LOVE'S GREETING (No. 55 *infra*,) which unites their voices in impassioned accents until, as if this motive no longer sufficed to express their ecstacy, it is followed by the MOTIVE OF LOVE'S PASSION (No. 56 *infra*,) which, with the Siegfried Motive, rises and falls with the heaving of *Brünnhilde's* bosom.

These motives course impetuously through this scene. Here and there we have others recalling former portions of the cycle—the Wälsung motive (p. 303, l. 2, bar 7), when *Brünnhilde* refers to *Siegfried's* mother, *Sieglinde;* the Motive of Brünnhilde's Pleading when she tells him of her defiance of *Wotan's* behest (p. 305, l. 2, bar 3); a variant of the Walhalla Motive when she speaks of herself in Valhall (p. 313, l. 3, bar 7); and the Motive of the World's Heritage with which *Siegfried* claims her, this last leading over to a forceful climax of the Motive of Brünnhilde's Pleading, which is followed by a lovely, tranquil episode introduced by the MOTIVE OF LOVE'S PEACE, which is succeeded (p. 319, l. 3, bars 1–5) by a motive, ardent yet tender—the MOTIVE OF SIEGFRIED THE PROTECTOR (Nos. 57 and 58 *infra*).

These motives accompany the action most expressively. *Brünnhilde* still hesitates to cast off forever the supernatural characteristics of the Valkyr and give herself up entirely to *Siegfried*. The young hero's growing ecstacy

55

(SIEGFRIED *in an outburst of the utmost rapture.*)
(SIEGFRIED *in erhabenste Enzückung ausbrechend.*)

O   Heil   der   Mut - - - ter,   die mich ge - - - - -
O   *hail   to   her   who   gave me to*

Molto largamente e pesante.

ff

molto tenuto.

Heil   der   Mut - - - ter,   die   dich   ge - bar!
hail   to   her........ who   gave thee to   life!

bar!   Heil
life!   *Hail*

tr   tr

f   p   f

finds expression in the Motive of Love's Joy. At last it awakens a responsive note of purely human passion in *Brünnhilde* and, answering the proud Siegfried Motive with

the jubilant Shout of the Valkyrs and the ecstatic measures of Love's Passion, she proclaims herself his. Then, as river and sea meet in turbulent billows, so meet the emotions of *Brünnhilde* and *Siegfried* in a surging flood of music.   As she clasps him to her bosom his frame quivers with a joyous thrill and in a glorious burst of impassioned melody love rises to its rapturous climax.   *Siegfried* and *Brünnhilde* are united!   From the Valkyr, fearful of surrendering her virgin purity lest with it she should loose her goddess-like power, *Brünnhilde* has changed to a woman, swayed by woman's emotions and passions and with that complete faith in her lover which is perhaps the most sublime attribute of woman's love.

The " Dusk of the Gods " is in a prologue and three acts.

THE PROLOGUE.

The first scene of the prologue is a weirdly effective con-
ference of the three gray sisters of fate—the *Norns* who
wind the skein of life. They have met on the Valkyrs'
rock and their words forebode the end of the Gods. At
last the skein they have been winding breaks—the final
catastrophe is impending. The chief Motives heard in this
scene are the Erda and Fate Motives, with which latter it
passes over to the second scene—*Siegfried's* farewell to
Brünnhilde.

An orchestral interlude depicts the transition from the
unearthly gloom of the *Norn* scene to break of day, the
climax being reached in a majestic burst of music as *Siegfried* and *Brünnhilde,* he in full armor, she leading her
steed by the bridle, issue forth from the rocky cavern in
the background.   This climax owes its sublime eloquence
to three motives—that of the Ride of the Valkyrs and two
new motives, the one as lovely as the other is heroic, the
former being the BRÜNNHILDE MOTIVE.(59), the latter
the MOTIVE OF SIEGFRIED THE HERO (60):

59

60

The Brünnhilde Motive seems to express the strain of pure, tender womanhood in the nature of the former Valkyr. This motive proclaims womanly ecstacy over wholly requited love, as distinguished from the barbaric frenzy of the wild horse-woman of the air, as *Brünnhilde* appeared to us in the first scene of the second act of " The Valkyr." The motive of Siegfried the Hero is clearly developed from the motive of Siegfried the Fearless. The fearless youth has developed into the heroic man. Its outburst from the orchestra in the dawn scene almost simultaneously with the first full effulgence of the day and the forthcoming of *Siegfried* and *Brünnhilde* from the cavern recall the psalmist's apostrophe of the sun:

Which is as a bridegroom coming out of his chamber.

It represents the highest development of manhood. It is the most exaltedly heroic and at the same time, if the expression be allowable, the most muscular motive of the Cycle.

In this scene *Brünnhilde* and *Siegfried* plight their troth, and *Siegfried* having given to *Brünnhilde* the fatal ring and having received from her the steed Grane, which once bore her in her wild course through the storm clouds, bids her farewell and sets forth in quest of further adventure. This scene is one of Wagner's most beautiful creations. In addition to the two new motives already quoted there occurs a third—the MOTIVE OF BRÜNNHILDE'S LOVE.

When a woman of a strong, deep nature once gives her-

self up to love her passion is as strong and deep as her
nature. It is not the surface-heat passion that finds expression in the French drama and the Italian opera to which
Wagner has given vent in the music of this scene. It is love
rising from the depths of an heroic woman's soul. The
grandeur of her ideal of *Siegfried*, her thoughts of him as a
hero winning fame, her pride in his prowess, her love for
one whom she deems the bravest among men, find magnificent expression in the MOTIVE OF BRÜNNHILDE'S
LOVE:

On p. 25, l. 2, bar. 2, occurs a contracted form of the
Motive of Siegfried the Hero which is effectively used
throughout the scene, especially in those portions where,
after Brünnhilde has given Grane into his charge, it is
heard in combination with the Motive of the Ride (p. 31,
l. 4, bar 3, and p. 33, l. 3, bar 2). On the page last quoted
this combination of motives is succeeded by a sturdy theme
—à bar from Siegfried's wander-song in the first act of
"Siegfried," which forms the basis of the impassioned
phrases with which *Siegfried* and *Brünnhilde* bid one another farewell (p. 36, l. 1, beginning at bar 2). *Siegfried*
disappears with the steed behind the rocks and *Brünnhilde*
stands upon the cliff looking down the valley after him;
his horn is heard from below and *Brünnhilde* with rapturous gesture waves him her farewell. The orchestra accompanies the action with the Brünnhilde Motive, the Motive
of Siegfried the Fearless, and finally with the theme of the
love-duet with which " Siegfried " closed.

The curtain then falls and between the prologue and the first act we have an orchestral interlude descriptive of *Sieg-fried's* voyage down the Rhine to the castle of the Gibich-ungs where dwell *Gunther*, his sister *Gutrune*, and their half-brother *Hagen*, the son of *Alberich*. Through *Hagen* the curse hurled by *Alberich* in the " Rhinegold " at all into whose possession the ring shall come, is worked out to the end of its fell purpose—*Siegfried* is betrayed and destroyed and the rule of the gods brought to an end by *Brünnhilde's* expiation.

In the interlude between the prologue and the first act we first hear the brilliant Motive of Siegfried the Fearless and then the gracefully flowing Motives of the Rhine, and of the Rhinedaughters' Shout of Triumph with the Motives of the Rhinegold and Ring. *Hagan's* malevolent plotting, of which we are so soon to learn in the first act, is foreshadowed by the sombre harmonies which suddenly pervade the music—the Motive of Renunciation (p. 44, l. 4) and a motive based on that of the Tarnhelmet and expressive of the NIBELUNGS' POWER for evil :

62

ACT I.

This act opens in the hall of the Gibichungs, on the Rhine. *Gunther*, *Hagen* (*Alberich's* son) and *Gutrune*, the sister

of *Gunther*, are plotting against *Siegfried*, of whose exploit
in capturing the ring from *Fafner* and freeing *Brünnhilde*,
Hagen knows. *Gunther* is disposed to be contented with
what he has, but *Hagen* urges him to take a wife and pro-
cure a husband for *Gutrune*, suggesting that she give *Siegfried* a love-potion, which will excite him to love her and
give up *Brünnhilde* to *Gunther*.

At the very beginning of this act the Hagen Motive is
heard. Particularly noticeable in it are the first two sharp,
decisive chords. They recur with frightful force in the
third act when *Hagen* slays *Siegfried*. The HAGEN MO-
TIVE is as follows:

This is followed by the GIBICHUNG MOTIVE, the two
motives being frequently heard in the opening scene :

Motives prominent in earlier scenes and easily to be
recognized occur when *Hagen* describes the beauty of
Brünnhilde, and the powers of *Siegfried* and suggests the
infamous trick by which *Siegfried* is to be induced to win her
for *Gunther*—the Motives of the Ride of the Valkyrs, of the
Wälsungs' Heroism (p. 49, l. 1, bar 4), of Siegfried the Fear-

less (p. 49, l. 3, bar 1) and of the Ring, Renunciation and Gold, followed appropriately by the motive of the Nibelungs' Power through which *Siegfried's* destruction is to be compassed (p. 51, l., 1, bar 2—l. 4, bar 1). Added to these is the MOTIVE OF THE LOVE POTION which is to cause Siegfried to forget *Brünnhilde*, and conceive a violent passion for *Gutrune* :

65

The notes of *Siegfried's* horn are heard in the distance. As *Hagen* looks down the river and describes to *Gunther* how, with an easy stroke, the hero forces the boat against the swift current, we hear an effective combination of the Motives of Siegfried the Fearless and of the Rhine-daughters' Shout of Triumph (p. 59, l. 1, bar 1); the Nibelung-son's boisterous greeting in answer to which *Siegfried* lays to with his boat is appropriately followed with tragic force by the Motive of the Curse. The Siegfried Motive imparts dignity to the meeting between the young hero and *Gunther*. When *Siegfried* asks *Hagen* how he recognized him although they had never met, the Motive of the Curse, prophetically significant, accompanies the query. At the hero's command to *Hagen* that he heedfully tend Grane the Brünnhilde Motive and the Motives of Brünnhilde's Love, and of the Ride of the Valkyrs are heard. After some parley between the men, *Gutrune,* who, at a gesture from

Hagen, had retired, re-enters bearing a drinking horn and approaching *Siegfried* bids him welcome in the GUTRUNE MOTIVE :

66

This is followed by the Motive of the Love Potion and then, after the orchestra has murmured memories of the love-scene in " Siegfried," the young hero drains the drinking horn to *Brünnhilde's* happiness. His manner suddenly changes. The Motive of the Love Potion becomes more animated. *Siegfried* regards *Gutrune* with growing admiration. He asks her of *Gunther* in marriage. The Love Potion, which he quaffed to *Brünnhilde,* has effaced all memory of her. This is made doubly apparent when *Gunther* asks in return for *Gutrune's* hand that *Siegfried,* disguised in the Tarnhelmet as *Gunther,* penetrate the fiery barrier and lead *Brünnhilde* as bride to him. *Siegfried* repeats mechanically, as if endeavoring to collect his thoughts, *Gunther's* references to the rock and fire, and even the mention of *Brünnhilde's* name awakens no responsive thrill in him. He offers to bring *Brünnhilde* to *Gunther* as bride and to unite himself with the Gibichung by the sacred compact of blood-brotherhood. Each with his sword draws blood from his arm which he allows to mingle with wine in a drinking-horn held by *Hagen;* each lays two

fingers upon the horn, and then, having pledged blood-
brotherhood, drinks of the blood and wine. This ceremony
is significantly introduced by the Motive of the Curse followed by the Motive of Compact (p. 75, l. 3, bar 5).
Phrases of *Siegfried's* and *Gunther's* pledge are set to a
new motive whose forceful simplicity effectively expresses
the idea of troth.   It is the MOTIVE OF THE VOW:

67

Blü - - hen - den   Le - bens   la - - - ben - des
Blos - - som - ing   life - stream,   lib - - - er - al

mf molto sostenuto.   *dim.*

Blut........   trän - felt'   ich   in   den   Trank.
blood........   drop - peth   in - to   the   drink.

Abruptly following Siegfried's pledge :

Thus drink I thee troth,

are those two chords of the *Hagen* Motive which are heard

again in the third act when the Nibelung has slain *Sieg-fried*.

Gunther and *Siegfried* enter the latter's boat, cast off and begin their journey to the Valkyr Rock where *Siegfried* under the influence of the magic Love Potion is to forcibly seize his own bride and deliver her to *Gunther*. The latter it should perhaps be stated here, is not aware of the union which existed between *Brünnhilde* and *Siegfried*, *Hagen* having carefully concealed this from his half-brother who hence believes that he will receive the Valkyr in all her goddess-like virginity.

When *Siegfried* and *Gunther* have departed and *Gutrune*, having sighed her farewell after her lover, has retired, *Hagen* broods with wicked glee over the successful inauguration of his plot. During a brief orchestral interlude a drop curtain conceals the scene which, when the curtain again rises, has changed to the Valkyrs' Rock where sits *Brünnhilde*, lost in contemplation of the Ring, while the Motive of Siegfried the Protector (No. 58) is heard on the orchestra like a blissful memory of the love-scene in " Siegfried."

Her rapturous reminiscences are interrupted by the sounds of an approaching storm and from the dark cloud there issues one of the Valkyrs, *Waltraute* who comes to ask of *Brünnhilde* that she cast back the ring into the Rhine and thus lift the curse from the race of gods. But Brünnhilde refuses :

> More than Walhalla's welfare
> More than the good of the gods,
>   The ring I guard.
> From love I part not in life,
> No gods can tear us asunder,
> Soon shall Walhalla's walls
>   Be dust for the winds !

It is dusk. The magic fire rising from the valley throws a glow over the landscape. The notes of *Siegfried's* horn are heard. *Brünnhilde* joyously prepares to meet him. Suddenly she sees a stranger leap through the flames. It is *Siegfried,* who through the Tarn-helmet (the motive of which, followed by the Gunther Motive dominates the first part of the scene) has assumed the guise of the Gibichung. In vain *Brünnhilde* seeks to defend herself with the might which the ring imparts. She ʹis powerless against the intruder. As he tears the ring from her finger, the Motive of the Curse resounds with tragic import followed by trist echoes of the Motive of Siegfried the Protector and of the Brünnhilde Motive, the last being succeeded by the Tarnhelmet Motive expressive of the evil magic which has wrought this change in *Siegfried. Brünnhilde's* abject recognition of her impotence is accompanied by the restless, syncopated rhythm of the Nibelungs' Malevolence (No. 22), as she enters the cavern. Before *Siegfried* follows her he draws his sword Nothung (Needful) and exclaims :

Now Nothung, witness thou, that chaste my wooing is ;
To keep my faith with my brother, separate me from his bride.

The music of this closing episode is forcefully graphic. It opens (*Piu animato,* p. 127) with the abrupt chords of the Hagen Motive. These and the Motive of Compact accompany the Sword Motive when *Siegfried* draws Nothung (p. 127, l. 2, bars 2 and 3). Phrases of the Pledge of Blood-brotherhood followed by the Brünnhilde, Gutrune and Sword Motives accompany his words. The abrupt Hagen chords lead to the Motives of the Nibelungs' Power and Tarnhelmet which pass into the Brünnhilde Motive. This rises for a moment triumphantly over the sombre, threatening harmonies of malevolence and sorcery. But it ends abruptly; and the chords so forcefully expressive of Hagen's vindictive power, with the Tarnhelmet Motive through which the thuds of the typical Nibelung rhythm resound, lead to the last crashing chord of this eventful act.

ACT II.

The ominous Motive of the Nibelungs' Malevolence introduces the second act. The curtain rises upon the exterior of the hall of the Gibichungs. To the right is the open entrance to the hall; to the left the bank of the Rhine, from which rises a rocky ascent toward the background. It is night. *Hagen*, spear in hand and shield at side, leans in sleep against a pillar of the hall. Through the weird moonlight *Alberich* appears. He urges *Hagen* to murder *Siegfried* and to seize the ring from his finger. After hearing *Hagen's* oath that he will be faithful to the hate he has inherited, *Alberich* disappears. The weirdness of the surroundings, the monotony of *Hagen's* answers, uttered seemingly in sleep, as if, even when the Nibelung slumbers, his mind remained active, imbue this scene with awful mystery. New in this scene is the MURDER MOTIVE:

68

A charming orchestral interlude depicts the break of day. Its serene beauty is, however, broken in upon by the MOTIVE OF HAGEN'S WICKED GLEE, which I quote, as it frequently occurs in the course of the succeeding events:

69

The Motive of Siegfried the Fearless accompanies
Siegfried's appearance. When *Gutrune* joins him and
Hagen, and *Siegfried* relates how he won *Brünnhilde* for
Gunther the Motive of the Tarnhelmet is frequently heard
usually combined with some other Motive, f. i., with the
Motive of Love's Joy at p. 144, l. 4, bar 1; with the Loge
Motive (p. 145, l. 3, bar 2) and with the Motive of the
Ride of the Valkyrs (p. 146, l. 1, bar 5). The appropriate
use of these will readily be recognized from the context.
Siegfried having led *Gutrune* into the hall, *Hagen* ascends
a rocky height and loudly summons the vassals of Gibich-
ung. During the ensuing bustling, noisy scene a variant of
the Gutrune Motive (p. 151, l. 3, bar 2) is employed as a
WEDDING SUMMONS:

A boisterous chorus of rejoicing, barbaric in its sturdy
force, greets *Gunther* as he leads *Brünnhilde* from the boat,
to the open space before the hall from which latter *Siegfried, Gutrune* and her train of women have issued. Soon,
however, the shadow of impending tragedy darkens the
scene.

When *Gunther* greets *Gutrune* and *Siegfried* with the Motive of the Wedding Summons, *Brünnhilde* raising her eyes
perceives *Siegfried* on whom her astonished gaze remains
riveted. The Motive of Siegfried the Hero, the Sword

Motive and the Chords of the Hagen Motive emphasize with a tumultuous crash the dramatic significance of the situation. There is a sudden hush—*Brünnhilde* astounded and dumb, *Siegfried* unconscious of guilt quietly self-possessed, *Gunther*, *Gutrune* and the vassals silent with amazement—it is during this moment of tension that we hear the motive which expresses the thought uppermost in *Brünnhilde*, the thought which would find expression in a burst of frenzy were not her wrath held in check by her inability to quite grasp the meaning of the situation or to quite fathom the depth of the treachery of which she has been the victim. This is the MOTIVE OF VENGEANCE:

71

Tenderly the Gutrune Motive, or rather the version of it which formed the Wedding Summons, accompanies *Brünnhilde's*

Siegfried here? Gutrune?

and *Siegfried's* calm response:

Gunther's mild-eyed sister
Mate to me as thou to him.

But it is broken in upon by the now unbridled fury of the Motive of Vengeance (p. 181, l. 3, bar 1). Then, again dazed and still incredulous, *Brünnhilde* totters and is saved from falling only by *Siegfried* who supports her. Looking up to him as she did when his being thrilled with love of her, she tenderly asks him, while the Brünnhilde Motive adds to the pathos of the scene, if he does not recognize her. Suddenly she sees the ring upon his finger. The crashing chords of the Ring Motive are followed by the Motive of the Curse. *Brünnhilde* now realizes the enormity of *Siegfried's* treachery—it must have been he, not *Gunther*, who overcame her. She hurls her accusation at *Siegfried* with versions of the Motive of Vengeance in which the wrath of injured womanhood seems to attain its most frenzied expression (p. 185, l. 3, bars 1 and 2; and p. 186, l. 1, bar 3 and l. 2, bar 1). When she invokes the gods to witness her humiliation the Walhalla Motive is heard. This is followed (p. 190, l. 2, bar 6) by the touchingly pathetic Motive of Brünnhilde's Pleading, which, however, soon gives way to the Motive of Vengeance when she calls upon the gods to give her vengeance commensurate with her wrong.

Brünnhilde accuses *Siegfried* of a threefold crime—of deserting her, of treachery toward *Gunther* in concealing from him that she had been his (*Siegfried's*) mate and of wronging *Gutrune* in wedding her when he had been already mated. *Brünnhilde*, knowing naught of the love-potion which has caused *Siegfried* to forget his night of love with her and to conceive a violent passion for *Gutrune*, thirsts for revenge upon him for his treachery. Her righteous wrath is intensified by jealousy of *Gunther's* sister for whom she believes herself to have been deserted. *Gunther* and *Gutrune* are also aroused, for *Hagen* carefully concealed from them all knowledge of the relations between *Siegfried* and *Brünnhilde*, and they believe that *Siegfried* exercised the nuptial privilege the night, when disguised as *Gunther*, he overcame *Brünnhilde*—that he has been unfaithful to *Gutrune* and has broken his vow of Blood-brotherhood with *Gunther*.

Siegfried takes oath that *Brünnhilde's* accusation is false ; *Brünnhilde* swears that it is true. The taking of the oath is introduced by the Motive of Vengeance.

Siegfried swears upon *Hagen's* spear. Hence the fitness of the Murder Motive and of the sharp, decisive chords of the Hagen Motive. As *Brünnhilde* takes the oath the Valkyr music courses through the orchestra. All her wild Valkyr nature seems unloosed. *Siegfried's* oath allays *Gutrune's* suspicions. The tension of the scene is relaxed by the glad measures of the Wedding Summons. *Siegfried,* throwing his arm around *Gutrune,* draws her joyously with him into the hall whither they are followed by the vassals and women.

Brünnhilde, Hagen and *Gunther* remain behind. The Vengeance and Murder Motives and the Motive of the Vow dominate the ensuing scene. *Hagen* offers to be the executioner of *Brünnhilde's* and *Gunther's* vengeance. Music and action fairly seethe with excitement. In a trio through which fierce, revengeful passions surge, *Brünnhilde, Hagen* and *Gunther* swear vengeance upon *Siegfried.* From this outburst of wrath they turn to behold *Gutrune's* bridal procession issuing from the hall. The valley of the Rhine reechoes with glad sounds—but it is the Murder Motive which brings the act to a close.

ACT III.

This act plays on the banks of the Rhine, where stands *Siegfried,* baffled in his pursuit of the game. *Hagen* has arranged that *Siegfried* shall be slain at a hunt and brought home as if wounded by a boar. While *Siegfried* stands on the bank of the Rhine, the Rhine-daughters appear to him and promise to bring game in his way if he will give them the ring. He refuses and they disappear, leaving him to his fate. For charming badinage this scene can be compared only with the opening scene in "The Rhinegold." The ripples of a lovely river do not exceed in grace the music with which Wagner has adorned this episode.

Distant hunting horns are heard. *Gunther*, *Hagen* and their attendants gradually assemble and encamp themselves. *Hagen* fills a drinking horn and hands it to *Siegfried* whom he persuades to relate the story of his life. This *Siegfried* does in a wonderfully picturesque, musical and dramatic story in which motives, often heard before, charm us anew.*

In the course of the narrative he refreshes himself by a draught from the drinking horn into which meanwhile *Hagen* has pressed the juice of an herb. Through this the effect of the Love Potion is so far counteracted that tender memories of *Brünnhilde* well up within him and he tells with artless enthusiasm how he won her. *Gunther* springs up aghast at this revelation. Now he knows that *Brünnhilde's* accusation was true.

Two ravens fly overhead. As *Siegfried* turns to look after them the Motive of the Curse resounds and *Hagen* plunges his spear into the young hero's back. *Gunther* and the vassals throw themselves upon *Hagen*. The Siegfried Motive, cut short with a crashing chord, the two murderous chords of the Hagen Motive forming the bass—and *Siegfried*, who with a last effort has heaved his shield aloft to hurl it at *Hagen*, lets it fall and, collapsing, drops upon it. So overpowered are the witnesses by the suddenness and enormity of the crime that after a few disjointed exclamations, they gather, bowed with grief, around *Siegfried*. *Hagen* with stony indifference turns away and disappears over the height.

---

* Nibelung, Sword, Dragon, Forest-Weaving, Tarnhelmet, Brünnhilde's Love, Brünnhilde, Magic Fire and Brünnhilde's Greeting.

With the fall of the last scion of the Wälsung race we hear a new motive, simple yet indescribably fraught with woe—the DEATH MOTIVE (p. 296, l. 4, bars 1 and 2).

Siegfried supported by two men rises to a sitting posture and with a strange rapture gleaming in his glance intones his death-song. It is an ecstatic greeting to *Brünnhilde*. "Brünnhilde!" he exclaims, "thy wakener comes to wake thee with his kiss." The ethereal harmonies of the Motive of Brünnhilde's Awakening, the Motive of Fate, the Siegfried Motive swelling into the Motive of Love's Greeting and dying away through the Motive of Love's Passion to *Siegfried's* last whispered accents—"Brünnhilde beckons to me"—in the Motive of Fate—and *Siegfried* sinks back in death.

Full of pathos though this episode be it but brings us to the threshold of a scene of such overwhelming power that it may without exaggeration be singled out as the supreme musical-dramatic effect in all that Wagner wrought and hence the supreme effect in all music. *Siegfried's* last ecstatic greeting to his Valkyr bride has made us realize the blackness of the treachery which tore the young hero and *Brünnhilde* asunder and led to his death; and now as we are bowed down with a grief too deep for utterance—like the grief with which a nation gathers at the grave of its noblest hero—Wagner voices for us in music of overwhelmingly tragic power feelings which are beyond expression in human speech. This is not a funeral march, as it is often absurdly called—it is the awful mystery of death itself expressed in music.

Motionless with grief the men gather around *Siegfried's* corpse. Night falls. The moon casts a pale, sad light over the scene. At the silent bidding of *Gunther* the vassals raise the body and bear it in solemn procession over the rocky height. Meanwhile with majestic solemnity the orchestra voices the funeral oration of the "world's greatest hero." One by one, but tragically interrupted by the Motive of Death, we hear the motives which tell the story of the Wälsungs' futile struggle with destiny—the Wälsung Motive, the Motive of the Wälsung's Heroism, the Motive of Sympathy and the Love Motive, the Sword Motive, the Siegfried Motive and the Motive of Siegfried the Hero, around which the Death Motive swirls and crashes like a black, death-dealing, all-wrecking flood, forming an overwhelmingly powerful climax that dies away into the Brünnhilde Motive with which, as with a heart-broken sigh, the heroic dirge is brought to a close.

Meanwhile the scene has changed to the Hall of the Gibichungs as in the first act. *Gutrune* is listening through the night for some sound which may announce the return of the hunt.

Men and women bearing torches precede in great agitation the funeral train. *Hagen* grimly announces to *Gutrune* that *Siegfried* is dead. Wild with grief she overwhelms *Gunther* with violent accusations. He points to *Hagen* whose sole reply is to demand the ring as spoil. *Gunther* refuses. *Hagen* draws his sword and after a brief combat slays *Gunther*. The victorious Nibelung is about to snatch the ring from *Siegfried's* finger, when the corpse's hand suddenly raises itself threateningly, and all—even *Hagen*—fall back in consternation.

Brünnhilde advances solemnly from the back. While watching on the bank of the Rhine she has learned from the Rhine-daughters the treachery of which she and *Siegfried* have been the victims. Her mien is ennobled by a look of tragic exaltation. To her the grief of *Gutrune* is but the whining of a child. When the latter realizes that it was

Brünnhilde whom she caused *Siegfried* to forget through the love-potion, she falls fainting over *Gunther's* body. *Hagen* leaning on his spear is lost in gloomy brooding.

Brünnhilde turns solemnly to the men and women and bids them erect a funeral pyre. The orchestral harmonies shimmer with the Magic Fire Motive through which courses the Motive of the Ride of the Valkyrs. Then, her countenance transfigured by love, she gazes upon her dead hero and apostrophizes his memory in the Motive of Love's Greeting. From him she looks upward and in the Walhalla Motive and the Motive of Brünnhilde's Pleading passionately inveighs against the injustice of the gods. The Curse Motive is followed (p. 326, l. 2, bar 4) by a wonderfully beautiful combination of the Walhalla Motive and the Motive of the Gods' Stress at *Brünnhilde's* words :

Rest thee! Rest thee! O, God!

For, with the fading away of Walhalla, and the inauguration of the reign of human love in place of that of lust and greed—a change to be wrought by the approaching expiation of *Brünnhilde* for the crimes which began with the wresting of the Rhinegold from the Rhine-daughters—*Wotan's* stress will be at an end. *Brünnhilde* having told in the graceful, rippling Rhine music how she learned of *Hagen's* treachery through the Rhine-daughters, places upon her finger the ring. Then turning toward the pyre upon which Siegfried's body rests, she snatches a huge firebrand from one of the men. Flinging it upon the pyre, which kindles brightly, she hurries toward Grane. As the moment of her immolation approaches the Motive of Expiation begins to dominate the scene (p. 333, l. 1, bar 2).

It wings its flight higher and higher until it seems to have soared to the height of emotional exaltation. *Brünnhilde* swings herself upon Grane's back, and with a mighty bound the steed bears his noble rider into the blazing pyre. Men and women in extreme terror crowd into the foreground. Suddenly the Rhine is seen to overflow, and borne on the flood the Rhine-daughters swim to the pyre and reclaim the ring. *Hagen* plunges madly after them into the flood and they draw him down with them. A deep glow illumines the heavens. It is the dusk of the gods. Walhalla is seen enveloped in flames. Once more the Walhalla Motive resounds majestically. But the Motive of Expiation breaks in upon it with overwhelming power. For the last time we hear the Siegfried Motive and then with the Motive of Expiation a new era—that of human love—rises in all its glory from the ruins of the empire of the gods.